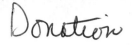

I glanced up into the woods, staring once more into vacant windows. The eyes and soul of a house no longer inhabited, at least not by anyone of this world. Voices whirled about in my mind. Lights have been seen in the cabin, after dark. Some say she doesn't rest at all, but walks at night. Then, from somewhere, the echo of a dog's plaintive howl sent icy fingers sliding down my backbone.

"I was here the other day," I said, my voice hushed. "I didn't know it was Cissy's cabin, but now I remember being here a long time ago, when the other kids were taunting her. It was awful, and I knew Gran would be upset with me. I think maybe she felt sorry for Cissy, or maybe she even knew her, before it happened."

"Before what happened?" Brendan drew next to me and leaned over to put his hand on mine where I gripped the reins.

I tore my gaze from the cabin and looked into his turquoise eyes. "The murder."

He considered this a moment before he said, "I think we should leave now."

Did he feel it too? The presence of someone other than us?

We did not talk at all as we rode away, but I couldn't resist a single backward glance at the lonely cabin. Strange how the breeze sifting through the trees now sounded more like someone's gentle sighing. Cecilia Jane.

Praise for Lucy Naylor Kubash

[The Haunting of Laurel Cove] received Honorable Mention in the ImaJinn a Romance contest.

The Haunting of Laurel Cove

by

Lucy Naylor Kubash

The Haunting of Laurel Cove

Cover Art by *Jennifer Greeff*

The Wild Rose Press, Inc.
PO Box 708
Adams Basin, NY 14410-0708
Visit us at www.thewildrosepress.com

Publishing History
First Edition, 2022
Trade Paperback ISBN 978-1-5092-4551-2
Digital ISBN 978-1-5092-4552-9

Published in the United States of America

Prologue

The cabin stands in the clearing near the Lazy River. I've not been there for some time now, not since the birth of my daughter; but one day when Althea is older, I will take her there, and I will tell her the story of the other two Altheas for whom she is named.

After much talking, I've finally convinced the inhabitants of Laurel Cove to restore Cissy's cabin as a historical marker, so it's not as ramshackle as it first appeared to me. My husband says I'm obsessed with the place. Maybe I am. I use to go there often, to stand in the overgrown herb garden with its brown and curling vines, to wander through the vacant cabin, to sit in the small, armless rocker and wait for the subtle fragrance of laurel to fill the room. But since the fateful day, it has not happened again. Cissy's cabin is quiet now and empty, save for the occasional tourist who cares to stop and have a look.

It's the way it should be, the way I wanted it to be, yet I sometimes wish I could feel her presence again, to remember how it felt to be touched by the spirit of Cissy Oliver.

It's strange how it all started when I came back to the mountains. Strange that Cissy's story once meant so little to me and was only a faded memory from my childhood, a memory left far behind in the mists of the Great Smokies. Now that I have set the story down it has become a part of me, just as the mountains are a part, and the two are inseparable in my mind—Cissy's story and the mountains—as inseparable as the blue smoke is from the high-tops of Clingman's Dome and Mt. LeConte...

Chapter 1

Morning mists had just begun to lift their veil from the mountains by the time I reached the Cove. All around me late spring splashed the meadows and verdant foothills with vibrant spots of color. Rhododendron and laurel bushes weighed down with pink and white blossoms lined the twisting road. I turned off the air conditioning and put the car window down to try and catch their elusive scent. The soft coo of a mourning dove drifted upon the sweet breeze, joined by the distant lowing of cows. How different from a year ago when I'd last driven this same road through Laurel Cove!

Mother and I had come to say goodbye to Gran and to attend her funeral. I recalled on the day of her service it was gray with fog and drizzle, as if the Cove itself mourned the passing of yet another of the old ones. My visit to the Cove then had been fraught with pain and sorrow, and when I'd left there'd been no plan to return again so soon. But this time I arrived with the hope a few weeks spent in the little hamlet tucked in the southeast corner of Tennessee would help me regain my badly shattered peace of mind.

Laurel Cove. Caught between the rolling green velvet of the foothills and the mistiness of the higher slopes, it remained a monument to a time forgotten, a time when folks lived simple, rural lives. Small family farms lay scattered across the rich valley that bloomed in

3

the shadow of the Smokies, and only the places catering to the tourists hinted inhabitants of the Cove bothered themselves at all with the goings on of the outside world. Of course, folks here were not untouched by everyday problems of the twenty-first century, but the illusion they were remained, and if you didn't know how to get here, it wasn't a place you would just stumble upon while driving through the mountains. Perhaps it was why so many chose to stay in the Cove, or at least to return from time to time.

"We'll be there very soon now," I promised my traveling companion. Pepper stood up and stuck her small black nose out the two inches of open window on her side. She snuffed at the air, eager to be out of the car. "It's been a long trip, I know, sweetie. I'm a little weary too." I stifled a yawn and shook my head to clear my vision.

It was then I first noticed the woman standing alongside the road. A slight figure, she wavered, as if unwell. It was no wonder. Despite it being nearly June, a black hooded cape cloaked the woman from head to foot.

I slowed the car to a crawl and, while driving past, I looked into her face. It surprised me when I saw not an old face but a very young one. She peered out from the folds of the hood, and I glimpsed a frame of abundant silvery hair and skin so fair it appeared almost translucent. Her lips trembled, as if she wanted to speak but could not. Yet her eyes spoke to me and held me so briefly in their trance. They were large, almost too large for her tiny face. I had never seen eyes so evocative…so luminous. I quivered looking into them and suddenly it was as though she beckoned me to stop.

Thinking perhaps she was in some kind of trouble, I

started to brake. I wasn't in the habit of picking up strangers, but after being a victim myself I couldn't resist this woman's silent plea. It was Pepper who stopped me.

My normally quiet, shaggy little Pepper suddenly let loose with a long pitiful howl.

"Hey, it's okay. What on earth is wrong with you?" I glanced away from the woman to try and silence the eerie serenade.

Confused, I kept driving but still felt a compulsion to help the strange woman. Glancing in the rear-view mirror, I expected to see her staring after me, but the sun suddenly beamed over the mountains and shone on the silver pavement, blinding her from my view.

The whole incident took place in only a few seconds, but it left me shaken. *Who was she?* What had she wanted, and why had Pepper reacted so strangely? Only the little dog's bizarre protest had prevented me from stopping. She whimpered.

I put out my hand to quiet her and noticed I was trembling. Why had the encounter with this woman affected us so? What about her had seemed so compelling?

I glanced in the rear-view mirror again. The woman was gone, but then I'd rounded a blind curve in the road so of course she would be out of sight. *If she had been there at all.*

What was I saying? Of course, she had been there. Maybe not as strange as I'd imagined her, but there! It was just the long hours of driving getting to me, fatigue making me think the woman had pleaded with me to stop, pleaded with eyes that had no color. Those eyes! I had not imagined them. They had been so real I could see them in my mind, shining out from the tiny, beguiling, sweet-sad face.

I shook my head, determined to rid myself of the haunting image. She was just a strange lady, that was all. No one to concern myself about.

In a few moments I spotted the twin sugar maples flanking the driveway to Gran's house. Someone had recently painted the white fence edging the yard, so it looked crisp and fresh. No doubt Uncle Theo had put in some extra hours over here. When I finally stopped in front of the two-story farmhouse, I shut off the engine of my sister's car, leaned back against the seat and sighed deeply.

"Well, here we are," I said to Pepper. She sat up again and looked inquisitively out the window. After her weird little spell, she'd settled down again, almost as if nothing had happened.

I unhooked her doggy seat belt and we got out of the car, stretched and spent a moment taking in the graceful old house. Built nearly a hundred years ago, it stood sturdy and strong, a testament to my ancestors' carpentry and Uncle Theo's maintenance skills.

Morning glories climbed the latticed trellis at each end of the wide porch, and lilac bushes drooped, heavy with deep purple blossoms. From the porch roof hung one of the wood and metal wind chimes my Uncle Theo made. A faint breeze from the mountains sifted through the leaves of the maples and set the chimes to tinkling in the delightful way I remembered from long ago.

This was Gran's house, the house where I'd practically grown up. I thought of old-fashioned rag rugs and crocheted doilies and sweet tea taken on the porch. Even after a year, it was hard to believe she was gone and the house now belonged to me.

The breeze brushed my forehead, and I ran my fingers through the new spiky hairstyle I wore. Just as my fingers touched the scar, I heard someone call out.

"Janey-girl, you made it."

The screen door slammed, and my aunt stood on the porch, dressed in one of her colorful sixties-hippy skirts and a white peasant blouse. Her long dark hair streaked with silver was caught up in a leather barrette.

Wiping her hands on a dish towel, she came down the porch steps, her rosy face lit with a generous smile.

"I thought you might not make it today. It's easy to get caught up in one of the summer traffic jams. Folks been swarming in around the park already. Did you come through Pineville? Was it hot driving? I just came over to open the house up for you. I air it out when I can, but we've been really busy lately."

Aunt Mattie always talked this way when she got excited, running her sentences together, barely giving you a chance to answer one question before she asked another. My mood lifted, and I went around the car to hug her.

When she engulfed me in her sturdy arms, Mattie smelled of flour and fresh-baked bread…and security. After a long moment, she held me away for her perusal.

"You sure you're all right, Janey-girl? You're looking a little peaked."

"It's been a long drive," I said. "I guess I'm just tired."

She scrutinized me and ran a gentle hand over my hair. To my aunt I would always be Janey-girl. It was the same pet name my father had once called me. In the past few years, I'd mostly thought of myself as C.J. Stuart, the author's name on my books. Lately, though, I

7

wondered who I really was.

With some effort, Mattie stooped to pet the wiggling Pepper. "Now who's this little scrap of fur? Your faithful companion?"

"Something like that." I watched Pepper clean Aunt Mattie's hand with an eager pink tongue.

"Well let's not stand out here in the day's heat, for heaven's sake. The big kitchen is nice and cool so let's have a glass of sweet tea."

She wrapped her arm around my shoulders and drew me to the house. "Are you hungry, girl? How about a sandwich? I stocked the refrigerator so you wouldn't have to shop for a while."

"Sounds good. I'll just get my things from the car."

"Never mind your bags, honey. Gil can fetch them in for you later."

"Gil? Gil Carson?"

"Sure enough. Your Uncle Theo hired him on this spring. You remember he was always a little slow, and he's had a few run-ins with the law, but he's trying to straighten himself out. We needed some repairs done on the cabins, so he and Theo struck up a bargain. Gil's pretty handy with a hammer and nails, and Theo and I aren't as young as we used to be, you know."

She told me all this while we entered the house with its blue chintz draperies and overstuffed furniture that spoke of a forgotten era. The house smelled slightly musty, though Mattie had opened windows to air it out, yet it wasn't so unpleasant. Once in the kitchen, I felt more at home, remembering all the family breakfasts eaten here so long ago.

Gran's kitchen. It looked like an ad from an eighty-year-old magazine. If Aunt Mattie hadn't insisted on installing a new gas range some years ago, the old black cookstove would no doubt still stand in the corner. Running water had been brought into the house long before I was born, but a pump handle reminiscent of the old days curved over the sink. Gran just never could give up her old ways, even to the end. She was buried in a plain pine box in the tiny graveyard, behind the church where she'd attended services all her life.

"So, how's the resort business?" I pulled out a ladder-back chair from the oak table and sat down while my aunt poured frosty glasses of sweet iced tea.

"Pretty much the same as always. We get a lot of the same folks back every year. We call them our regulars. And there're always a few new honeymooners. Some of them become regulars and eventually come back with their families."

While not exactly a flourishing business, Singer's Resort was a landmark in the Cove. Theo and Mattie had taken it over when Gran could no longer manage the place alone, and with no children of their own, they'd dedicated themselves to the business and made it their life.

Mattie opened the refrigerator. "Ham salad okay? I brought over a jar of bread and butter pickles, too. You always were fond of them."

"Sounds wonderful."

She fixed me a plate and joined me at the table with her tea.

"We've done a lot of remodeling in the cabins this past year. Althea never wanted us to change anything. She seemed to think folks liked them just the way they were, but Theo and I know to keep people coming back you've got to make some changes. Sticking to the old ways is fine in some things. I sell my quilts, and Theo carves his wind chimes. City folk love to take something from the mountains back home with them, and it's a little extra income for us. But competition is fierce nowadays. We put air-conditioning units in the cabins, and we're hoping to get Wi-Fi service set up. You got to give people what they want."

I took a long drink of sweet tea and let it slide, cool and soothing, down my throat. Then I stared down at the homemade bread Mattie had filled with her famous ham salad. For the first time in weeks, I was actually hungry.

"Aunt Mattie, tell me the truth." I had to ask the question. "Am I city-folk?"

She eyed me in her quizzical way, then her face slowly broke into a wide grin, lighting her hazel eyes with warm affection.

"Maybe in some of your ways," she said and patted my shoulder reassuringly, "but not in your heart, Janey-girl, not in your heart. Now eat up."

While I filled my stomach and my spirit in Gran's kitchen, content as I'd not been in a long time, Aunt Mattie offered Pepper a bowl of water and a chopped hot dog. The little dog's whole body wriggled her thanks.

"One night a week we serve a big homestyle dinner for the folks staying in the cabins." Mattie talked while I ate. "Nothing fancy, just plain good food, but they enjoy it."

"Must be a lot of work for you." I sampled a pickle slice and savored its spicy sweet-sour taste.

"It is, but work's never been a stranger to me. Women in these parts have never lacked for something to do."

So true. I remembered Gran, busy from morning

until night, always at some chore that needed tending. Running the resort was no small job.

Mother had not been one to do it, nor my sister Maureen. They had simply not been of the same mold as my father's family, the Stuarts. But what about me? Did I still fit in, or was I now just an interested onlooker?

"More ice tea?" Aunt Mattie raised the foggy pitcher above my glass. I held it up for a refill.

When a light knock sounded on the back door, Mattie called out, "C'mon in, Gil."

The "boy" Aunt Mattie had spoken of was somewhere in his late-thirties by now. I recalled he'd always been different, slow moving, slow talking. His parents had kept him home, refusing to send him to school, but they had been gone for some years now. I wondered how he looked after himself. By his appearance, not very well. Baggy brown pants and a faded plaid shirt hung on his spare frame. Greasy hair stuck up in stiff little tufts, and a grizzle of beard stubbled his weak chin.

"You remember my niece, don't you Gil? It's Jane. She's down here from New York for a little visit." I was glad she didn't mention the real reason for my coming back to the Cove. "Her daddy was my twin brother, and they all used to live here in Laurel Cove before Jack died, but it's been a long time ago."

Indeed, it had been fifteen years since my father had died and my mother, a transplanted Yankee, had taken Maureen and me back north to live. Perhaps it was the reason for my hesitation when Gil extended his hand to me. Years of city living, and especially the incident three months ago, had left me instinctively wary, and though I knew Gil to be harmless, it was all I could do not to shrink from his friendly gesture. When I finally did accept it, his hand felt large and clammy.

"How ya doin', Miss Jane?" He nodded his head. I glimpsed tobacco-stained teeth, or what was left of them, and fought the impulse to recoil again.

"Have some tea, Gil?" Mattie handed him a tall glass, taking his attention from me. I wondered if she'd noticed my reaction. Little escaped my aunt's sharp eye. She had a way of seeing everything, even if she offered no comment at the moment.

"Thanks." Gil accepted the glass and drained the contents in one long swallow, the gulping motion making his Adam's apple bob up and down. "That's right good." He smacked his thin lips and set the glass down.

"Did you finish replacing the screen in the cabin?" Aunt Mattie went back to the sink.

"Yes, ma'am, I did. She's all fixed now. Won't no more mosquitoes and moths get in there tonight." Again, he flashed his brown-toothed grin.

"Good. I'd like for you to do me one more favor, and then if Theo doesn't need you anymore today, you can go."

"Sure, what did ya need?" He spoke to Mattie, but his eyes remained on me.

"Janey's bags are out in her car. I'd like for you to bring them in for her and take them on upstairs. She's going to be staying over here."

For some reason, I wished she hadn't told him I'd be here alone. When Gil started for the door, I jumped up to follow.

"I'll unlock the trunk, and there's no need for you to carry them all." I turned back to my aunt. "I think I'll go upstairs and get settled anyway."

"Fine with me, honey. Take yourself a nap. Supper won't be ready 'til six-thirty. You come over when you're ready." She left then to return to her own house just down the road. I was left alone with Gil.

"No need to help me." Gil shook his head when we stood by the car. "I can carry your things."

"It's okay. I have a lot." And I thought it better if I carried my new laptop. It was the first thing I'd replaced of my vandalized possessions, and I'd brought it with me in hopes of being able to better concentrate on writing once in the Cove. My editor had graciously given me a generous extension on my latest manuscript, but I suspected my career as C. J. Stuart, author of young adult paranormal mysteries, rested on getting myself back to normal—and finishing the book—as quickly as possible.

I allowed Gil to take my rolling duffle bag and the one with Pepper's food and treats. I grabbed my backpack containing the laptop and the briefcase containing my printed manuscript pages written so far.

"Mattie said for me to help. Maybe I should take those." Gil stared at the several other bags in the trunk.

"It's okay," I murmured. "I'll get them later." I led the way back to the house.

"You can leave the dog food in the kitchen," I said and glanced around, wondering where Pepper had gone. Off somewhere exploring, no doubt, and certainly she was safe here.

Once upstairs and at the door of my old room, I told Gil to set the duffle bag down. Hand on the doorknob, I waited for him to leave. I just didn't want him to watch me go into my room.

"I can manage from here. Thanks for your help."

"Oh-okay. 'Bye Miss Jane." He gave me a lopsided

grin.

"Thanks again." I watched him shuffle away while a strange mixture of guilt and apprehension rippled through me. I waited until he'd descended the stairs and left the house before running back down to retrieve the rest of my things and haul them upstairs. Then I opened the door to the room where I'd slept so many years ago.

Once all my bags were inside, I shut the door and looked around, my gaze lingering over all the details I recalled so clearly now.

In the far corner stood the cherry wood wardrobe. Not far from it, the matching highboy and vanity. The walls were still papered in a tiny violet pattern and along the front of the room, opposite the door, three wide windows looked down on the entire front yard. Aunt Mattie must have opened them. Sheer white curtains floated in and out with the breeze.

My eyes went to the polished oak floor. As a child, I'd loved to walk barefoot across it, just to feel its satiny smoothness. As if answering some deep need in myself, I slipped off my sandals and went to stand next to the object that was my favorite in the room—the cherry wood four-poster bed. Once it had seemed so high and safe, a haven from the world. My hand trailed over one of the solid posts and across the lacy white coverlet. Gran had crocheted it for me for my twelfth birthday.

I had treasured this gift, so why had I left it behind? Perhaps because I'd not wanted to separate it from this room, this house.

I sank down on the bed. I'd always slept so well here, snuggling in early with one of my favorite books and a big bowl of popcorn for company, completely content. It would be nice to snuggle in right now and let it comfort me, but sleep had not come easy these past few weeks. I doubted it would find me now.

When I'd hung the few skirts and dresses I'd brought in the wardrobe and folded lingerie, jeans, shorts, and t-shirts in the highboy, I arranged my cosmetics neatly on the vanity and put my earrings into Gran's little wooden jewelry box. Then I pulled the vanity stool up in front of the windows, perched on it and leaned my elbows on the sill. The view from this room was nothing less than spectacular.

Rolling fields, dotted with bronze bundles of hay, swept away to meet the velvety green foothills. Sloping gently, they soon became one with the misty peaks of the higher ranges. The breeze, rich with the mountain fragrance, drifted in and I breathed it, relaxing in a way I'd not thought possible anymore. Just to sit at these windows, just to survey the gentle yet rugged mountains was to know a sense of peace and serenity hard to find anywhere else. There was no denying it. Coming home had been good for me. Already my appetite had picked up, and perhaps, with the help of the four-poster, I might even be able to sleep the way I once had, before the attack.

Resolutely, I pushed all unpleasant thoughts from my mind. Instead, I thought about something that had been playing at the back of my mind since I'd stepped into this house today. It had to do with Gran and the last time I'd been in the Cove.

My grandmother had been thin and frail a year ago, but her eyes had burned with a fiery spirit. Even now I recalled how she looked at me that last time and what she said.

"Someday Janey-girl, you'll come back. Someday.

The mountains, they'll keep callin' you. They're in your blood, and there's a reason for you here...a purpose...and it will be waiting...'til you come back."

No one understood what the old lady was talking about. Mother tried to convince me it was just the rambling of a senile mind, but I remembered, and I knew now, as I'd known then, there was nothing senile about those flashing eyes. Gran had known what she was saying and to whom she was saying it, but I had yet to figure out to what she had referred. What would be waiting? This room? Possibly. Except for the curtains, no changes had been made since I was a girl. It was almost as if the room had been left as it was precisely for my benefit. So when I did come back, I would feel as if I still belonged. So I might discover the purpose. *Purpose!* What possible purpose could I have in Laurel Cove? The only reason I'd returned now was because of what had happened in my apartment late one February night.

Back to that again. Rising from the window, I returned to the four-poster and this time I accepted its invitation. Stretching out across the lacy coverlet, I sank into the soft folds. They molded to fit me, and in a few moments, I sank into the deep sleep I'd needed for so long.

It was nearly six when I awoke. Somehow, Pepper had managed to join me and was curled up at my feet. I glanced at the now open door. Had I done that? *Huh, must have before I laid down.*

"You're as bad as I am," I murmured and scratched behind Pepper's floppy ears. While she slumbered, I got up and went to take a bath in the old claw-footed tub. Refreshed, I slipped into a yellow flowered sundress and white sandals. A light touch of makeup and I was ready to join Theo and Mattie and their guests for dinner.

Chapter 2

Pepper refused to be left behind.

"You have to promise not to beg," I said and opened the car door. I could see Mattie and Theo's bungalow from here and considered walking over, but it was nearly six-thirty. I didn't want to be late.

"I hope you don't mind I brought her," I said in Mattie's kitchen, enticing Pepper into a corner with a doggy bone. "She's not used to staying alone in strange places, but she'll stay in here if she knows I'm nearby."

"Not a problem, Janey-honey," Mattie said, and before I left the kitchen, I saw her slip Pepper a hand-out.

Mattie served supper in the sun porch off the kitchen. A bright, cheery room paneled in knotty pine, it showcased more of Theo's wind chimes and a daisy print quilted wall-hanging.

A small rocker sat in the corner, empty. When visiting, Gran had always sat there and for a moment I imagined the fiery old woman, rocking and crocheting, her fingers always busy.

A sudden catch gripped my throat, but a dear and familiar voice cut through the nostalgia and brought me back to the present.

"Hey, Janey-girl, it's good to have you back." Uncle Theo took my hand in both of his gnarled ones.

Blinking away a tear, I put an arm around his neck

and hugged him soundly.

"Thanks, Uncle Theo. It is good to be home." I kissed his softly wrinkled cheek and his moustache curled up at the tips tickled me. His hair, silvery white, was tied back in a ponytail. His flannel shirt was faded but neatly pressed, tucked into equally faded jeans. Mattie and Theo were children of the sixties. I stood off to look at him. "Ah but you're just the same," I said. "The years never touch you at all."

He smiled in his easy way. "Can't say the same about you. Use to think for a while there you were going to grow into some long-legged filly instead of a young lady, but you're a beautiful woman, Janey-girl. We were just so sorry to hear what happened to you. Are you all right now?" A wealth of concern welled in his eyes, and though I had no desire to talk about the incident, I appreciated his caring.

"I'm fine," I lied and let him guide me to a place at the table.

Theo seated me next to another familiar face, Jedidiah Hamilton. I knew from Mattie's occasional emails Jed still owned a local hardware store, was the unofficial mayor of Laurel Cove, and Theo's official fishing partner. The two had been cronies for more years than either cared to count. We exchanged only a few pleasantries before dinner guests began crowding into the sun porch, eager to sample my aunt's culinary fare.

They had good reason. Even Theo admitted Mattie had outdone herself with the night's menu. There was southern fried chicken heaped high on three large platters, scalloped potatoes, golden cornbread cut in squares, fresh glazed carrots, and corn on the cob dripping with melted butter. For dessert, a choice of peach cobbler or blueberry pie. Throwing all cautions to the wind, I took some of everything.

"I thought Aunt Mattie said she serves simple meals." I marveled at how she had managed all this cooking by herself.

"Well, it isn't everyday a member of your family comes home." Uncle Theo winked at me. "It's for you, Janey-girl, she's gone all out. She's so glad to have you back."

I was thankful to be taken back with open arms. Perhaps a little time spent in the serenity of Laurel Cove was exactly what I needed.

After the guests left, I started to clear the long table and carry dishes to the kitchen. Mattie would hear none of it. She shooed me out with the flick of a dishtowel.

"Go sit on the porch and keep Theo and Jed company."

I knew better than to argue with the woman. Pepper and I went out to the front porch and sat in the swing where the heavy scent of lilacs filled the summer twilight and silent mists stole down from the shadowy mountains. Sitting on the steps, Theo and Jed talked quietly. Lulled by the gentle motion of the swing and the hum of night creatures, I caught only a few words of their conversation, but in the back of my mind I had the passing notion they were words unfamiliar to folks who lived in Laurel Cove. Hotel complex, condos, golf course, development.

Before I could make sense of it, the excitement of the day took its toll on me. I knew if I didn't go back to Gran's house soon, I would have to be left curled on the swing all night. It was as if my body now craved the sleep it had been denied for so long.

"Guess I'll call it a day." I stood and stretched and went to pat Theo's shoulder where he sat on the top step. "It's been a long one. Tell Aunt Mattie good night for me, would you?"

"You sure you'll be all right over there by yourself? You know you're welcome to stay here with us. Just because Althea left you the house doesn't mean you have to occupy it. If you'd rather not be alone…"

"Thanks for the offer, but it's okay, really. I'm used to being by myself, so it doesn't bother me." Or at least it hadn't until a few months ago. But surely, I would be safe in Laurel Cove, in Gran's house.

"It's good to see you again, Jane." Jed tipped his baseball cap to me. "You going to be here long?"

"Few weeks."

"Then I'm sure I'll see you again."

I drove back to the farmhouse, glad I had remembered to leave a light on.

Before heading up to bed, I made chamomile tea and curled in the corner of the sofa with the steaming mug. Pepper jumped up next to me and glanced about the strange house. "I know it's hard, sweetie," I sought to soothe her and myself, "but we have to get used to being alone again. We can't be paranoid forever." She rested her head on my arm and I stroked her ears, wondering if she really did remember the night we'd come home from our evening walk and startled the intruder. Did she recall the terrifying moment when he'd come at me with something…something he'd bashed down on my skull? Luckily, there was no fracture, but a severe concussion and gash had kept me hospitalized for several days. It was still tender where nineteen stitches had closed the gash, the reason for my new short hairstyle. Pepper had tried gallantly to protect me, but a well-landed kick to the ribs had put her out of commission, too. It was perhaps what angered me the most. My own injury was hard enough to accept, but that the creep had viciously attacked my little dog made me burn.

"We'll be fine," I promised her. "This is Laurel Cove. Nothing can hurt us here."

I wanted desperately to believe this, but when I undressed in my room a little later, I froze at a sudden soft scuffling sound. I'd left the windows open for air and the sound came from outside. Standing there half-naked, I could not make myself move. What if someone was on the porch? Gil knew I was here alone. What if he'd come back? I heard it again, a rustling in the bushes, and Pepper growled low in her throat.

Snatching up my nightshirt, I threw it on and forced myself into action. Inching toward the window, I peered out from behind the filmy curtain, straining to see the yard below.

The trees cast dark shadows across the lawn, and I could only see a corner of the porch from my room. I studied the lilacs, smelled their perfume heavy in the Tennessee night. Were those bushes moving? I held my breath.

A moment later I exhaled in relief and even laughed as a small cotton-tailed bunny hopped away from the porch. Rabbits had always made burrows under the porch. Gran had fought for years to keep them out of her garden. Probably fifty generations of rabbits had lived beneath the porch. I sighed deeply.

"But I'll be right back," I told Pepper and ran downstairs to make sure I had locked both front and back doors.

Once in bed, I read for a while and finally managed to sleep. I slept well until sometime in the dawning hours I began to dream. It wasn't like any of the dreams I'd been having in recent weeks, of coming into my trashed apartment and finding the trasher still there. This dream was a peaceful one of me driving through the Cove, looking out on picturesque farms and churches, horses and cattle grazing in lush pastures, and a silver road clear in front of me. Only suddenly, it wasn't clear anymore. Now it was marked by the small figure of a woman dressed in a long dark robe. The same woman I'd seen on the way into the Cove. I'd almost forgotten about her.

Once again, I slowed down and caught a glimpse of her fair face. It seemed so tormented. At some peculiar noise, she faded away before I stopped and she had a chance to ask me…*to ask me what?*

I woke with a start and found the strange noise a part of reality. A storm had brewed over the mountains and peals of thunder rumbled across the valley. I leaped from the four-poster to shut the windows against the rain already pelting down.

Back under the sheet, I tried to shut out the storm and return to sleep, but it was no good. With the advent of the rain the room turned oppressively hot, and soon I couldn't bear even the sheet. I tossed it back and lay for a moment staring up at the plaster ceiling with its hairline cracks, unable to toss off as easily the aftereffects of the dream. It hadn't frightened me, but there was a curious feeling about it and what had actually happened on the Cove road. I couldn't figure out either one.

About the time the storm spent itself and the sun inched over the mountains, I rose to begin my first full day back in Laurel Cove.

It was going to be a hot one, made even more humid by the rain. I dressed in cut-offs and a blue sleeveless blouse and went barefoot downstairs.

I had just brewed a cup of tea when Aunt Mattie knocked at the back door. In one hand she held a covered plate, in the other, a jar of homemade strawberry jam.

If she noticed I had to unlock the door before letting her in, Mattie didn't comment.

"Well, you're up early. Thought maybe you'd sleep in this morning." She came in and set the overflowing dish on the table. When she uncovered it, I glimpsed sausage patties, hash browns and fresh biscuits. Hearty breakfasts were a tradition in the Cove.

"The storm woke me, and I couldn't go back to sleep. My goodness, Aunt Mattie, you didn't have to do this for me. I'm sure you've got enough to do at your own house." I wondered if I should tell her about the dream and the incident that prompted it. Maybe she would know the identity of the strange woman.

Mattie motioned for me to sit and drew up a chair across from me. Flour powdered the front of her blue-checked apron, and some of the dust had settled on her silver-streaked hair, but her hazel eyes shone warmly for me.

"Don't deny your old aunt of pampering you a bit. You and Maureen were my brother Jack's babies, and when I never had any of my own, I doted on you two. Come on now, eat up. You need to regain your strength."

I smiled and spread butter, a royal extravagance, on a biscuit. "You and Daddy were close, weren't you? I guess it must have been hard for you when he died."

"It surely was, he was my twin, but it was really hurtful when your mother insisted on taking you girls up north. I guess she just couldn't stay here without him, but then when she remarried, we figured the ties would be cut for good."

"There were a lot of times I wanted to come back," I said softly, staring at the biscuit. "But Mother promised me if I stayed, I'd have the best education, wherever I wanted. That was important to me."

"Of course it was, honey. I don't blame you."

"But Gran did. When I came down to see her before she died, I really didn't feel I even belonged here anymore."

"What nonsense. Of course, you belong. More than either your mother or sister, you were a true part of the Cove. Just like your Daddy. Your Gran knew that, and it's why she left you the house."

I smiled at her and sipped my tea, and we chattered on about lighter things. Then I asked her about my lady of the road. "She was so strange, Aunt Mattie, almost pathetic. Who do you think she was?"

My aunt didn't seem particularly surprised. "Though we are out of the way, a lot of unusual characters come through the Cove. Something about the mountains attracts the eccentrics. Always been that way, and it's no doubt that is who your dark-robed lady was."

An acceptable enough solution to my question, yet in the back of my mind, why did I feel there was more to it?

After breakfast I insisted Mattie let me clean up.

"Well, I won't argue with you." She turned an eager eye to the sunlight pouring through the kitchen window. "I've some gardening to do, and I would like to work on my quilt for a while. It's an old log cabin pattern. I'm planning to enter it in the art and craft show in Pineville

25

next month."

"Then you go ahead. I'm fine."

She touched my face briefly, her hand brushing my hair where it barely covered the pinkish-red scar.

"If you need anything, anything at all, you give us a holler. Promise?"

I nodded.

"I'll just put this away for you." She picked up the jar of jam and had opened the refrigerator when a light knock sounded on the back door. Trusting soul that she was, she didn't bother to ask who it was but just called out her cheery, "C'mon in."

Probably Gil, I thought and turned to the stove to pour another cup of tea. I was adding honey to it when the screen door opened and shut softly, and then someone who sounded nothing at all like Gil said, "Good morning."

Startled at the deep male voice, I wheeled about splashing tea and sticky honey down the front of me. "Oh...my...good morning," I stammered and flushed and stared across the kitchen into a pair of brilliant turquoise blue eyes. In place of Gil, there stood just inside the door a man whose presence filled even this large room. He smiled in a way that was unnerving, as if he silently laughed at me. Flustered, I grabbed a dishtowel and tried to mop the tea dripping down my arm.

"I'm sorry," he said. "Did you burn yourself?"

"No...no, the tea was only lukewarm." I made a few useless swipes at the stains on my shirt. "And you didn't startle me. I just thought it was Gil coming in."

I heard his low chuckle and glanced at him across the kitchen. This time I noticed more than just the color of the man's eyes. He was tall, several inches over six feet I guessed, and well-built. Like Gil, he didn't care much about his clothes. His jeans were faded and denim shirt rumpled, but the way they fit him made all the difference in the world. His sleeves were rolled carelessly back to reveal sinewy forearms and his collar lay open against the heat. His shoulders were wide and chest broad, reminding me of a solid wall. Yet it wasn't his ruggedness, nor the amused lift of his mouth that bothered me. It was, of all things, the distinct color of his hair. It waved away from his forehead, a rich, deep shade of red-brown, almost the color of burnished mahogany. In the brief instant I stood taking all this in, I had the strangest notion somewhere, at some time, I had known this man.

I searched desperately for something to say, wondering why he didn't just speak up and say what he wanted. Mattie saved me from further embarrassment. Hands on her wide hips, she stood looking from me to the man and back again.

His gaze shifted to my aunt. "Good morning, Mattie. Seems I inadvertently startled your niece, and she spilled her tea."

Something about the way he spoke, half-mocking, piqued my temper. Yet even in my reaction there was familiarity. Why? And how did he know I was Mattie's niece? Had she told neighbors I was coming home? Word had a way of spreading through the Cove in no time flat, so it wouldn't be surprising if the whole valley knew Jane Stuart was back.

"Do you mean to tell me," my aunt shook her head in disbelief, "you don't remember this fellow?"

I looked up blankly. I did…but I didn't. I wasn't sure.

"Now I know it's been a while, but I didn't think a body could forget someone she practically grew up with, especially someone like Brendan."

"Brendan?" Realization began to dawn. "Brendan McGarren?"

"In person." He grinned again in his flippant way, tilting the red-brown head to one side. "Just a few years older, but not necessarily wiser."

I couldn't believe it! Brendan McGarren, the boy who had once taken endless pleasure in teasing me about being a bookworm. Brendan, whose whole life had revolved around hiking up in the mountains. Brendan, the tall lanky youth, once the bane of my teen-age existence, stood before me now, a grown man.

"Jane, honey, have you gone and lost your tongue?" My aunt waved a hand in front of me.

I came to and shook my head absently. "No, I...please forgive me. It's just I never expected to see you, or for you to look so..." My voice trailed off, and he seemed to know precisely what I was thinking. With a rumbling laugh he crossed the room and held out his hand to me. I put my own into it and was astonished at how it engulfed mine. I simply couldn't say a word.

"It's good to see you, too, Ceely Jane," he said when I just stared.

I flushed irritably at him and myself. Brendan was the only person to have ever used a shortened version of my first name, Cecilia, and I truly hadn't heard it in many years. "It's been a long time," I murmured, which was quite the understatement.

"It has at that." He held my hand just a trifle longer than was necessary. His warmth traveled up my arm.

"But it *is* good to see you." Then, as if sensing my

discomfort, he released my hand but not before adding in a low tone, "You've changed some too, but I would have known those big brown eyes anywhere."

Brendan always did have a way of thoroughly disconcerting me, and the years had not altered that one bit. He could still make me feel foolish as a blushing thirteen-year-old.

Content he had teased me enough for now, he turned to Mattie, handing her what I'd not even noticed he was holding in his other hand, some sort of aromatic roots wrapped in wet paper towels.

"Oh, the ginseng roots!" She took them and seemed very pleased. "I hoped you would bring them around."

"Theo said I'd find you over here. I would have brought them sooner, but I've been up to the mountains the past couple days. I dug those fresh from my patch this morning."

"Been doing some hiking, have you?" She turned to dampen the paper towels again.

He nodded, absently rubbing a finger across his bearded chin. "I'm running a two-week seminar for some of my more ecology-minded students this summer. We'll hike part of the Appalachian Trail and do some strenuous backpacking, so I thought I'd check out a few of the trails. Had to make all the necessary arrangements with the rangers, too."

"Brendan's a teacher now," Mattie explained. "He teaches biology over at the high school in Pineville. He's also our most vocal advocate for environment protection. Head of a local group dedicated to the cause."

"Why am I not surprised?" I said, having recovered some degree of aplomb. "You always were more concerned about frogs and birds and going up to the mountains than anything else." I had to get in my own dose of teasing now.

It seemed as children, and even later as teens, we'd always been at odds with each other. I loved the mountains, but books had my first allegiance, leading the brash Brendan to dub me with the slightly scoffing title of "intellectual." For him, the mountains had been his life. I wasn't surprised to learn they still were. What did amaze me was that he had seen fit to stick with school long enough to become a teacher.

"And I hear your love affair with books is going strong." His eyes danced with mischievous turquoise lights. "Mattie tells me you're a published author now, writing as C. J. Stuart. She said your books have really taken off. Sounds pretty impressive."

I shrugged. "I'm not sure how impressive it is, but my teen fans love them."

He pulled out a chair and straddled it, leaning his arms negligently along the back. "Turned into a regular workaholic, have you? If you don't mind my saying so, you look like you're in need of a rest. You've come to the right place, anyway. The mountains are considered by some to have remarkable restorative powers. But of course, you ought to know. You grew up here."

Why did I detect a certain sarcasm in the remark? We hadn't been around each other for ten minutes and already I could sense the friction.

As if he knew my discomfort, Brendan turned to my aunt and changed the subject. "I saw Gil heading for the hardware in town. What's Theo got him doing today?"

"I think he's set to fix the fence out back and paint the shed. I suppose they needed some more nails and paint and such."

"It's really decent of Theo to give Gil the work. Not everyone around here would, you know."

"Well, he deserves a chance. It's not his fault he's like he is or that his folks didn't see to some kind of decent education for him. He doesn't have any family left now, since Jed's wife, his aunt, passed away. And she did ask Theo and me to look out for Gil when she was gone."

I didn't think it was why they'd given him the job, and if it was a handyman they needed, they could have done better. It was simply Mattie and Theo's way to give someone a chance. Gran had been that way, too.

"We're all weak in one way or another," Mattie said. "Folks tend to forget we've all got our Achilles' heel. But now where are you going so soon, Brendan? Sit back down. How about a biscuit and some nice strawberry jam?"

He declined and held up his hand. "No, but thanks just the same. I'm due over at the school shortly. We've got some planning to do for the hiking trip, and I have a meeting with the kids later today. Lots of stuff to get down pat."

He opened the screen door and was about to bid us goodbye when Mattie halted his exit. "Did you say you were up around Mt. LeConte the last few days?"

He turned back towards us. "I didn't, but yes, that's right."

"Was the laurel blooming yet?"

He lifted a puzzled brow. "Near reached its peak a little early." He sounded as if he wondered what Mattie was getting at. She knew as well as he exactly when every type of wildflower and shrub bloomed.

"I was just thinking." Mattie glanced in my

direction. "If I remember rightly, Janey was always rather fond of the mountain laurel, weren't you honey?"

"I was." I drew the word out, suspicious now myself.

"Then it might be nice if you could take her up to see the laurel slicks real soon."

Her words hung in the air, and I was aware of his turquoise gaze fastened on me. What had just happened here? Whatever Mattie had up her sleeve, I was certainly not going to play that game, not even for her. I could take myself up to see the laurel just fine and opened my mouth to say so, but he spoke first.

"If you like, but we'll have to go soon or you'll miss the fullest bloom."

Why the protest died before passing my lips I didn't know, but suddenly the chance to see the lovely pink and white laurel slicks was just too inviting, even if it meant going with Brendan. Besides, he had always known some of the best trails.

"If it wouldn't put you out any," I hedged.

He shrugged one shoulder. "It wouldn't."

"Then...yes, I'd like to go."

A flicker of surprise passed over his face, quickly replaced by—what was it—indifference?

"I'll let you know when we can go. See you ladies later."

With the slam of the screen door he left, before I could say another word.

My aunt clicked her tongue and gave me a doubtful look. "You haven't changed any where he's concerned, have you?"

"Well, he hasn't changed either." I turned to washing up my few breakfast dishes. "He's the same old

Brendan. *Ceely Jane*. He knows I always hated that nickname."

I glanced up and caught the roll of Mattie's hazel eyes, the hint of a grin. "Janey-girl," she said. "If you can look at that man and say he's not changed since you saw him last, then honey, you're mighty blind."

My face grew warm. "I wasn't speaking of appearances, Aunt Mattie." But what she said was true. The tall, broad-shouldered man who had stood in the kitchen a few moments ago bore little resemblance to the lanky, smooth-faced youth I remembered. Except for his hair, of course. In my life, I had yet to see another person with hair quite his color. Like fine polished wood, it had shone in the morning sunlight.

Chapter 3

"What do you say we go for a walk?"

Pepper sat up and yawned indolently.

"Now surely you can muster more enthusiasm," I chided. "The Cove is a nice place to walk. Besides, we need the exercise." We'd had precious little of it lately.

I went up for her leash and paused to put on my running shoes and change the tea-stained blouse for a red t-shirt. Downstairs I managed to coax Pepper out the screen door. Once outside she became a bit more agreeable, wagging her plumy tail and perking floppy ears.

The morning had grown exceedingly warm and the mountains steamed under the bright sun. A silver haze rolled down their velvet slopes, but the lure of the woods beckoned me to search for the path I knew led from Gran's house to the river road. All about us the valley burst with life, and life seemed sweet, especially now that I knew the terror of looking possible death in the face.

We found the path, overgrown with weeds but still visible, snaking through the field behind Gran's house. Wildflowers bloomed freely everywhere. Cornflowers, as blue as the spring sky. Tiger lilies, splashy orange. Sweet clover, a carpet of pink. I felt an intangible joy to revel in their delicate beauty. Years ago, on lazy summer days, Maureen and I had often fashioned wreaths for our hair from yellow-eyed daisies and Queen Anne's Lace and spent many an afternoon riding a nearby farmer's fat ponies, pretending we were princesses living in a far-off kingdom.

The dirt road bisecting the back of Gran's property led directly into the woods. The sun poured down like warm honey, making the shade of chestnut oaks and sweet buckeye an invitation I couldn't resist. The two-track meandered through the woods to the Lazy River, a rushing stream of water that was anything but lazy and flowed straight out of the mountains into the Cove. Always deliciously cold, the river's quieter green shallows provided a refreshing place to wade.

Tall trees immediately blocked the sun, and the air smelled damp and fertile. Glad to be out of the hot sun, Pepper pranced along, ears perked and nose lifted to take in all the new sounds and scents. Like a retreat, the woods settled down over us. Shy violets bloomed here in secret and small creatures scuttled beneath the lacy ferns. A calm repose should have filled my heart, but the dark woods also reminded me of the stories Gran used to tell about the elves and fairies, goblins and gremlins who abided in these woods. Sometimes called the Cherokee Little People, Gran had often used tales of those spirits to frighten two playful children into the house at night.

Thinking about them gave me a sudden chill and then something, I was never sure what, took my attention. In the middle of the narrow road I stopped, turned, and looked up.

From the cover of the forest, vacant windows stared back at me. It was only a shell of a house. A small cabin whose roof sagged and chimney crumbled into itself, the chinking falling away from between the logs.

It seemed at once a lonely little house, and yet somehow endearing, as if it had been left too soon to molder away in these woods, uncared for and unwanted. Weeds and wildflowers refused to grow around it, leaving the small area in front of the slanting stoop covered only with brown scrubby grass.

It wasn't a place that warranted a closer look, yet it's exactly what I wanted to do, suddenly had to do, as if I were inexorably drawn to it.

The suddenly balky Pepper halted my steps. The stubborn little animal plunked herself down and refused to be budged.

"All right then, just stay put." I wrapped the end of the leash about a small stump and set off alone through the shadowed woods, determined to have a closer look at the forlorn cabin. Did I remember it from my childhood? Who had lived here?

For the second time in as many days, Pepper stopped me from following through on an impulse when she threw her head back and howled like one possessed. The eerie sound froze me in my tracks. It was just like yesterday in the car.

I went back to her. "What is it, sweetie? What's getting into you lately?" I crouched down and hushed her with soothing fingers. "I was only going to have a look. I wasn't abandoning you."

It didn't seem to matter, and as Pepper whimpered and looked from me to the cabin, I had the strangest notion she saw something I didn't. Then she did something that made my skin crawl. Just like the night we'd come home from our walk and surprised the burglar in my apartment, the hair on her back rose and she let go with a long, low, rumbling growl. It came from deep within and vibrated against my hand. Goose bumps sprang up on my arms.

"There's really no reason for this," I tried to sound nonchalant to calm her as well as myself, but it didn't work and she continued to growl. "Okay, if it will make you happy, we'll just finish our walk."

I picked up Pepper's leash, and when she saw I had no intention of going closer to the cabin followed along obediently. But as we walked away, I ventured a glance over my shoulder. In spite of the howling and my skin tingling, I wanted to go closer, to peer through those empty windows, to know what was inside.

At the river, Pepper waded into the shady shallows and lapped up the water with appreciative gusto. Peeling off my shoes and socks, I joined her, gasping at the chilly temperature.

How many times had Maureen and I done this as kids? The Lazy River had always been enjoyed immensely by Cove residents and visitors alike. The sports-minded sought to try their art at angling for trout; other more daring souls brought inner tubes to ride the rapids. Some crazies just leaped in, without the tubes, from the high banks lining the river farther on. Summer weekends saw it jammed with tourists, and I supposed it was only because this was the middle of the week that Pepper and I had the spot all to ourselves today.

Returning to the mossy bank, we stretched out beneath the trees. Looking up through their dizzy heights, I rested and watched the way the sun played peek-a-boo through the broad oak leaves. It was peaceful and hypnotizing, and I very nearly fell asleep, but the plaintive coo of a mourning dove sent a shiver along my arms. I sat up with a start, then laughed. Once the haunting sound had been as familiar as my own breathing, but life had taught me some hard lessons. I'd learned not to be too sure of anything but to be wary of what might be lurking just around the corner—like a thief in my apartment.

I watched the river flow and wished it could sooth me as it once had many years ago, but though the water traveled serenely here, less than a mile downstream the rapids ran quick and rough. The joy of the tube riders. The death of someone who fell in and was swept along by the current against their will.

I put on my shoes and picked up Pepper's leash. This time, when we walked down the road, I didn't look up the path to the cabin, didn't look into empty windows that beckoned like seeing eyes.

I stopped in at the resort and found Mattie in the office, trying to both answer the phone and take care of guests. And there was lunch to put on the table for Uncle Theo and Gil.

"What can I do to help?" I asked.

Mattie didn't hesitate to hand me her reservation book and point to the phone. "Just take care of this for a while. Seems like I've been on the phone nonstop the last two hours." She hurried away, obviously glad to escape the jangling contraption. I settled myself on the high stool behind the desk and for the next hour took reservations. In between calls, I talked with folks who wandered in and out for one thing or another.

Bent over the reservation book, I didn't even hear Gil come into the office. When he spoke, I jumped and dropped my pen.

"Mattie keepin' ya busy?"

Glancing up, I saw him standing just inside the door,

smiling at me with his slightly vacant expression. It was, of course, silly to feel so uneasy around him, and I made up my mind then and there to be friends with Gil, to overcome my reluctance.

"Was there something you wanted, Gil?" I forced my voice to sound pleasant.

"Just come to say lunch is ready."

"Thank you. I'll be there shortly." I slid from the chair and looked about the floor for the pen.

He stepped behind the desk and held out his hand to me. "Ya lookin' for this?"

I reached for the pen but couldn't repress a shudder when he pressed it against my fingers.

"Somethin' wrong?" His narrowed eyes watched me as a cat's might.

"Just a sudden chill." But what a silly thing to say when the air-conditioner in the office wasn't working and the room was sticky-hot as the breathless air outside. Beads of perspiration stung my upper lip and my hair curled against my forehead damply. For a moment I met Gil's gaze, then quickly pretended to have some business with the cabin keys hanging on the wall.

"Tell Aunt Mattie I'll be right there," I excused him.

"Yes ma'am," his drawl slid over the words.

I heard him shuffle away and was relieved when the door slammed shut.

At the table, it was almost impossible to eat with Gil sitting across from me, but I could hardly move away.

"Quit picking at your food," Mattie scolded. "That walk you took should have revved up your appetite, not squelched it."

"I guess it's just the heat." I speared a tomato in my salad and took a small bite. It wasn't quite a lie—New

York was not nearly so warm yet—but it wasn't the reason for my discomfort. I would have been fine had every time I glanced up, I'd not seen Gil staring at me.

"So where did you walk today?" Uncle Theo asked, and I was grateful for his distraction.

"We just took the old road down to the river and came back." But that wasn't all. Between the house and the river there had been something else. The cabin. Should I mention it? Perhaps Theo might know who had lived there.

"I did see something in the woods, an old deserted cabin. It looked pretty decrepit, but it seemed like I should remember who lived in it. Should I?"

I gazed thoughtfully out the sun porch window. What had I felt while looking at the cabin? A sense of deja vu. Perhaps, as a child, I'd walked past it on my way to the river. Yet, there was something else about it.

"Flowers and weeds grow all around it, then they stop just like that, and the stoop is bare." My voice took on a peculiar, absent quality, and I could see the cabin so clearly in my mind. Everyone else in the room seemed very far away. "It was so forlorn, so empty. I wanted to go closer, but something…something stopped me." I shook my head, trying to remember. Suddenly, part of it seemed vague. What had kept me from going closer to the cabin?

I saw Pepper lying in the corner and frowned. "It was Pepper," I said slowly, starting to remember again. "She was howling and for no reason. She just didn't want me to go near it. I don't know why."

I looked around the table. Everyone had fallen silent. Theo and Mattie exchanged a puzzled expression.

"Did you walk up to it?" Mattie finally asked.

"No, I didn't. Pepper was setting up enough ruckus to wake the dead and—"

Gil choked on his soup. Mattie hurried around the table to pat him on the back. "Take it easy, son. You eat too fast."

Only I didn't think that was why he'd choked. Gil hadn't been eating fast. Gil didn't do anything fast. I'd said something to disturb him. What was it?

"Sun gets pretty hot down here." Uncle Theo went on eating. It can get to animals as well as people, and your little Pepper isn't used to it."

"I suppose you're right." I tried to put aside the vague feeling of curiosity troubling me. "It's just…there was something so elusive about it all. I can't put my finger on it." For a moment fear gripped me. Had the blow to my head caused some lasting damage after all? Perhaps it had taken several months to show up, and now I was losing my grip.

No! I refused to believe it. The doctor had said I was fine. *I was fine.* But then why had I been so compelled to go to the cabin?

"There just seemed something familiar about this cabin, like I could remember being there before."

Mattie smiled sympathetically and once she made sure Gil was all right, she took her seat again. "As I think about it, I believe I know why you felt that way. I'm surprised you don't remember, but I guess the years away from the Cove have made you forget a lot of things."

I thought of this morning, when a certain man came into the kitchen. Could the old cabin once have been as familiar to me as Brendan?

"Why should I remember, Aunt Mattie? Whose

place was it?"

"Cissy Oliver's," she said quietly.

A flicker of memory stirred. *An old woman. A woman who lived alone, the subject of adult suspicion...and children's taunts.* She never went into town but only puttered around her cabin, tending her cats and her strange garden. The garden. Had it been the reason for the ridicule and the fear? I remembered now a patch of odd-looking plants, mostly herbs, and used for what purposes was anybody's guess. The children of Laurel Cove had dared one another to gather on the road and taunt the old woman. Witch Cissy they had called her.

"Cissy's cabin," I murmured, the memory flooding me now and sending a chill prickling down my backbone. "I was always sorry for her." Because she was different, eccentric. But there was more to it than her just being strange. There was another reason Cissy was an outcast.

"Why did kids make fun of her, Aunt Mattie?" I suddenly had to know. "Was she really so strange?"

"Looks like you've got some story-telling to do this afternoon." Uncle Theo pushed away from the table. "Seems our Janey-girl has forgotten a lot."

"But you eat up first," Mattie insisted, offering more food to me. "Nothing but skin and bones, and I don't intend for you to stay that way."

I obeyed but my mind remained on the cabin and the woman who had once lived there.

"Don't know if I'd go wanderin' around the old place," Gil advised when he got up to follow Theo. He'd recovered from the choking incident and his gaze once again settled on me in his disconcerting way.

"Why not?" I forced myself to ask.

"I heard the place is haunted. People seen lights dancin' in the windows."

"Oh Gil, that's just a lot of nonsense." Mattie, ever practical, brushed off the idea.

"Just repeatin' what I hear. Some says it's just folks tryin' to keep them big business fellas from movin' in the Cove."

I noticed a frown slip over Mattie's jovial features. Without another word she began to clear the table. When Gil shuffled out the door, I turned to my aunt.

"What did he mean by that?"

She ignored my question and said only, "Let's put these dishes in the washer and go sit on the porch a while."

When we'd settled there, Mattie at her quilting frame and me in the swing, I asked again about Cissy Oliver.

"I didn't know the whole story myself 'til one day not long before your Gran died." While she talked, Mattie's deft fingers stitched at the colorful log cabin pattern. "She was the one who told me, almost like she suddenly had to. She was a young wife when this happened, but she was sharp in recalling it to mind, and she was bound and determined to tell me, though I couldn't see why. Folks didn't bother much with old Cissy anymore, not even the kids. The whole legend about her had kind of died out, except among the old-timers. But your Gran insisted I know all of the story. Mighty strange how she was so set on it."

Mattie stopped her work for a moment and stared off into space.

"What was the story of Cissy?" I gently urged her

on.

"Hmmm? Oh yes, the story." She brought herself back from wherever she'd drifted and began stitching again. "As your Gran told it to me, it went something like this." Her nimble fingers were busy again, and she kept her eyes on the intricacies of the quilt pattern, but her voice took on the lilting cadence of an old storyteller as she handed the legend down to me.

"It was said Cissy Oliver was one of the prettiest babes ever to be born in Laurel Cove. As a child, she was the light of her folks' life, for they weren't young and Cissy was their only child. But even as a little one misfortune came to Cissy. Her folks, the both of them, died in a typhoid epidemic and she was raised by an old maiden aunt. The aunt died when Cissy was a young girl and about that time a traveling preacher man came through the Cove with his family. When they left, they took Cissy with them because there was nobody else to care for the girl.

"They saw to it she got schooling, and she proved to be a smart girl. Some years later she came back to the Cove, teaching certificate in hand, her head full of ideas about bringing better education to the children here. She took herself a small cabin not far from the Lazy River and began to teach school in the church house.

"Now Cissy had grown into a beautiful young woman. She was said to be quite lovely, but in a whispery, fair way. She was shy where it came to men, having lived most of her life with first a maiden aunt and then a preacher's family, but she hadn't been back in the Cove long before she had enough beaux to make any girl's head spin, let alone one as innocent as Cissy. It was her very innocence that proved to be her undoing. With all the young men of the Cove to choose from, it was to Cissy's eternal misfortune she let the reckless Sheridan O'Malley catch her eye…and her heart. The name Sheridan itself means wild man, and wild he was reputed to be. An adventure seeker, and it was said there was nothing he wouldn't try at least once. But he had one redeeming quality, and it was Cissy's downfall—his Irish looks. Dark of hair and blue of eye with a smile as beguiling as sunshine on the mountains, there was never a handsomer man come into the Cove. Whatever Sheridan did he did in a grand way, and so he courted Cissy with a fervor she had never known. Having been orphaned at such a tender age, she'd missed much of the love due a child, and when the charming Sheridan turned his smile on Cissy, she fell for him and soon would see no other man.

"They courted all that spring, and it was said he promised to wed her when the laurel bloomed. It was her favorite flower, and Cissy wanted to wear a wreath of it in her hair for her wedding day. But tragedy struck again.

"Not long before the marriage was to take place, Sheridan was found in the woods, dead, a single bullet shot straight through his heart. He was laid out by the river, not far from Cissy's cabin, and when the sheriff found him, there was a bunch of pink laurel blossoms lying across his chest, covering the bloody spot where the bullet tore through.

"Now everyone in the Cove knew what a ladies' man Sheridan was, and there was no reason to believe he'd changed his ways just because he was betrothed to Cissy. It was also well-known to the school children their teacher's favorite flower was the delicate pink laurel. Wasn't long before the finger of suspicion turned on

Cissy."

For the first time, I interrupted the story. "But why would she want to kill the man she loved?"

"Plain and simple, honey," Mattie's voice became her own again, as if she had not really been the one telling the story at all. "The old green-eyed monster. They said Cissy found out Sheridan was seeing other women, and here they were about to be married. She'd never dealt with such a thing before, and the poor girl just went out of her head and shot the man dead as they walked along the river one night. A few days after Sheridan's burial, which Cissy never attended, they brought her in for questioning, but they couldn't find the gun and couldn't prove she did it. They had to let her go. But as far as folks of the Cove were concerned, she was guilty. Even if they figured Sheridan had it coming to him, murder was still murder. Then there was the fact Cissy wouldn't speak up, wouldn't say a word one way or the other if she was the one to silence forever the handsome wild man's reckless laugh."

"And nothing ever came of it?"

Mattie shook her head. "Cissy went back to her cabin and withdrew from life in the Cove. She became the recluse we all knew."

"But I remember the children calling her a witch." My mind grappled to recall the terrible little chant the children had sung.

"The notion she was a witch just kind of grew up over the years. She always wore those long dark robes, and her hair grew so silvery past the middle of her back. She tended her herb garden, and had cats following her around. Folks called them her familiars."

"Maybe she was just lonely. She had to have

something for company. As for the garden, how many women in the Cove don't have an herb garden they tend faithfully? Even you."

My aunt shook her head ruefully. "I really don't know the reason, or even if there was one. Folks here believe what they want to believe, and even to the day she died, there were a few who liked to believe Cissy had strange powers. When they heard what the doctor found, they were just all the more convinced."

A tiny breeze stirred the wind chimes and they tinkled a strange tune. I hugged my arms and suppressed a shiver. "What did he find, Aunt Mattie?"

"A group of hikers on the way to the river saw Cissy lying face down in her garden. She was already dead. Nobody even really knew her age, but when the doctor at the morgue got all those long robes off her, he found her body to be as slim and straight, her skin as clear and smooth as a young woman's. It was as if Cissy hadn't aged a bit since Sheridan O'Malley was killed, except for her hair, of course. But it was said to have changed soon after Sheridan's demise. It wasn't just any old drab gray, though, but more of a shimmering silver, as if the moon itself was caught up in it. Those who believed she was a witch said this was proof, her body not aging."

I leaned back in the swing and sighed. "Poor Cissy. She couldn't find justice even in death. And for folks to believe she was a witch. I should think her dying would prove she wasn't one. Witches aren't supposed to die, are they? And what did Gil say about lights in the cabin?"

Mattie seemed reluctant to speak on this and when she did her voice was hushed. "I guess some folks don't believe she's gone at all. Some say even now, she walks about that old place of hers."

My skin prickled as it had when Pepper howled, and I stopped the swing from moving with the toe of one sneaker.

"What about you, Aunt Mattie? What do you believe? Have you ever seen the lights?"

She stopped stitching and her gaze met mine. "I haven't gone looking. Seems bad enough they called poor old Cissy a witch, now she's a ghost too. I know some people think us folks from Laurel Cove are a suspicious lot, and in some ways maybe we are, but I think we should all just let this woman rest in peace. I'm sure she had enough grief in her life."

I went back to swinging for a while, remembering the uncanny interest the cabin had held for me only a few hours ago. Even now, I had the urge to go there again. In spite of the sometimes-spooky books I wrote, I wasn't sure I believed in ghosts or witches either, but something about the cabin drew me to it.

"Aunt Mattie, did I ever go to Cissy's cabin as a child?" I asked.

Mattie glanced up. "I wondered if you'd remember. It wasn't something your mother approved of. Your Gran took you and Maureen there a few times when you were just tots. She was always bringing Cissy food, but Jack put a stop to her taking you girls when your mother had such a fit."

Perhaps that explained my strange fascination with the cabin, but try as I might I couldn't recall what Cissy had looked like. I almost asked Aunt Mattie, but one of the guests came up looking for a hiking map. When she rose to get one, I knew our conversation about Cissy had ended for now. Yet I had one question left to ask.

"How long has it been since Cissy died, Aunt

Mattie?"

She hesitated, then said softly, "Why, it was three months ago yesterday."

I gasped softly. Three months ago yesterday, I had suffered the attack.

Chapter 4

The rest of the day I sat at the kitchen table, laptop open and my latest work in progress on the screen. But I barely squeaked out two pages before restlessness took over. Not even my usual ploys of promising myself a chocolate reward if I finished a chapter would work. I answered a few text messages from Maureen and my editor Lydia, but with no bars on my phone, who knew when they'd go through. Spending time on social media wasn't even an option, and I hoped my chatty teen-age fans wouldn't forget about me and find another favorite author. Yet somehow, I didn't really seem to care. Today, I needed to be outside doing something physical.

Pepper and I wandered back to the resort and found Aunt Mattie working in the herb garden behind the house. The warm, fertile fragrance of newly turned earth drew me.

"Need help?" I asked.

"Not if there's something else you need to do." Mattie glanced up from beneath her bright poppy red hat.

"There's not," Working in Gran's garden had always been a thing I enjoyed.

"In that case, grab a pair of garden gloves off the back porch."

I passed up the offer of the gloves and went right to work with a small spade, turning up the rich dark soil.

"I haven't had dirt under my fingernails in a long

time," I told my aunt ruefully. The few potted plants in my apartment were dumped by the burglar. "Believe it or not, this actually feels good."

I held some of the sun-warmed soil in my hand, savoring its lush scent. I knew Mattie was watching me, but she said nothing, simply smiled in a way that told me she understood.

As we worked, she began to chatter on, telling me about the plants Brendan had brought her just this morning.

"We've had our own patch of ginseng for a long time. Guess just about everybody around here does, but I'm replacing some plants damaged by disease. It takes two years for ginseng to come up from seed. It's a slow-growing plant but long lived if left alone to mature. You dig the roots in the spring only to transplant them into another bed, like these. Aside from that, you dig only in the fall when the berries are ripe. Some folks don't care when they dig, which is why 'sang in the wild is slowly dying out. Too many found out 'sang gathering could be profitable. It brings a high price, and most of it comes right out of these mountains. I'm telling you, it's a good thing we all got our own patches, too, 'cause there's no telling how long you'll be able to find it up here." She nodded toward the hills, her hat brim bobbing. "And I don't know what your uncle would do if he didn't have his 'sang roots to chew when his stomach gets to bothering him. He swears by it, and I myself like to drink a tonic of it every now and then. It strengthens the digestion. Maybe you ought to try a bit of it, Jane-honey. Might build you up."

Although some might laugh at Mattie and Theo's belief in the benefits of ginseng and other natural herbs,

I knew faith in many folk medicine remedies was a mountain tradition. I wouldn't scoff at it. I remembered too well Gran's dosing us with one of her homemade tonics every spring.

Pleasantly tired that night, I found my eyes drifting shut almost as soon as I settled in the four poster. Drowsily, I switched off the lamp on the nightstand and with a sigh sank back against plump down-filled pillows. It was a blessed relief for sleep to come so easily. Just before drifting off, I glimpsed filmy white curtains floating against the open windows and caught the fresh sweet scent of laurel and lilacs and early summer mountains.

Sleep came on a peaceful note but didn't remain that way for long. I began to dream again, this time about the cabin, the one where Cissy Oliver had once lived.

Buried in my mind lay the taunting song the children of Laurel Cove had once sung to torture the poor old woman. While awake, the words had eluded me. In sleep, they spilled out of my subconscious like a torrent too long imprisoned.

"Witch Cissy, Witch Cissy, say she killed a man.
Witch Cissy, Witch Cissy, name was Sheridan.
Witch Cissy, Witch Cissy, the wild man spoiled her love.
Witch Cissy, Witch Cissy, she hunted him in the Cove.
Took a gun and in his heart put a shot clean through,
And if you don't watch out, she'll put a spell on you!"

I had stood once with those children, listening as they sang the silly yet frightening little chant. I remembered not wanting to join in and putting my hands over my ears to shut out their sing-song, high-pitched voices, hating myself for even coming with them. Hadn't Gran told Maureen and me time and again not to join in this vicious if popular game? Desperately, I wished I'd gone riding, or walked to the river, anywhere I wouldn't be able to hear their awful words.

Now I was a child again, standing on the narrow path, staring at the lonely little house shadowed by the woods, thinking about what some of the kids said about the old woman who lived there, that she truly was a witch and could turn us all into toads if she so chose.

Then the object of all the taunting appeared, and the children dispersed, their false bravado shattered by the "witch's" appearance. Only I was left to stand on the path, as if truly in a spell. I met her gaze across the clearing and could not break away.

Held by the anguish, the emptiness, and desolation in the fragile face, empathy surged through me and also a strange connection. But fear proved a greater emotion, and at a shout from the others, I broke away and fled, grateful to be putting as much distance as possible between myself and those unrelenting eyes.

As I raced down the dusty road, I swore to myself never to come this way again, never to take this path to the Lazy River. The promise had remained unbroken— until today.

I jerked awake and lay with my eyes wide open, heart pounding, my mind unable to separate dream from reality. I was fully conscious, but the dream remained. I could hear those voices chanting, could see the pathetic figure of Cissy Oliver standing in the cabin doorway.

Suddenly the room held an eerie coolness. I touched

my forehead and found it damp. Was it the last vestige of the dream clinging to me making me shiver, or the sight of filmy white curtains floating in the summer breeze? Nearly an hour passed before I slept again.

The aftereffects stayed with me all morning. I simply could not chase from my mind the figure of the lonely old woman. She had invaded my sleep and for some strange reason would not leave my thoughts now. But why after all these years should I be so concerned with her?

Something Mattie had said the day before bothered me. Gran had insisted on telling her Cissy's story before she died. Why had it been so important to Gran that someone know? And why did it somehow all come back to me?

There could be no immediate answers to my questions, and in an effort to shake off this peculiar mood, I decided to go to work on the flower beds in front of the house, to clear away the spiky horse nettle taking over where marigolds and sweet alyssum once bloomed. This time, I scrounged about and found a pair of gloves to battle the prickly weeds. While I launched an attack, Pepper lay on the porch drowsing in the summer heat.

I'd been working for some time, pausing only to brush away the perspiration trickling down my face, when she suddenly woofed and a tall shadow fell over me. With a start I looked up and saw Brendan. He towered over me where I crouched in the dirt, and even against the glare of the sun I could see the amused grin that split the red-brown beard.

"Do you always sneak up on people?" I demanded.

"No. Sorry if I startled you, but you looked so earnest, yanking at those weeds, I hated to disrupt you."

"Well, you did," I stated and sat back on my heels. Peeling off the gloves, I wiped sweaty palms on dirt-stained jeans.

"Yes, I suppose I did." He rubbed a finger slowly over his beard. "Well, so long as you're already disturbed, how about we drive up to see the laurel today?"

"Right now?" I looked in dismay at my grubby attire. "I'd have to clean up."

"Then let's get moving. Morning is the best time in the mountains, you know. It will be hotter as the day goes on."

He was talking down to me, as if I were some ignorant tourist, and I didn't appreciate it at all. Leave it to Brendan. He had been standing here for all of five minutes and already he had me irritated.

He tipped his head to one side and the sun glinted off his hair, giving it a burnished sheen. As if to avoid being blinded by the fiery thatch, I looked away. Even as a young girl the color of his hair had fascinated and disturbed me. Perhaps because I thought it wasted on a man, especially when mine was such an unpretentious brown.

"It really is a fine day for a drive," I heard him say. "Only a few clouds on the high-tops."

Did I detect a hint of eagerness for me to say yes? I glanced up and saw he'd extended a hand to me.

"Coming?"

I almost allowed him to pull me up, but some little goblin from the past interfered. Ignoring his gesture, I got to my feet.

"Give me a minute." I gathered my gloves and garden tools. "I'll be right down."

He settled himself on the porch steps to wait. Before I went inside, I saw Pepper sidle up to him and rest her head on his arm. He obliged her by scratching behind her ears.

"Thanks a lot," I grumbled. Inside, I washed my hands and face and ran a hasty comb through my spiky hair. Clean jeans and a pink t-shirt took the place of the soiled ones, and I added a light touch of make-up. I was only going for a drive through the mountains, not out on the streets of New York, but taking pride in my appearance was one scrap of dignity I'd clung to these past months. Thank goodness I no longer needed heavier makeup to hide the ugly bruises.

In the yard, I saw Brendan talking to Gil. Being around the handyman still made me nervous, and I'd managed to avoid him so far today. I had no desire to face him now and stepped back inside to make sure Pepper was settled with a biscuit. When I came out again, Gil had gone. I went to climb in Brendan's four-wheel drive.

He slid in behind the wheel, his tall body accommodating itself to the small space. "All set?"

I nodded but he waited, then he asked, "Is something wrong?"

"It's just…Gil. Something about him…disturbs me."

Brendan's laughter rumbled along with the four-wheel drive's engine. "Now there's somebody you don't have to worry about. He's harmless."

Maybe so, maybe I was being silly, but I couldn't seem to change my attitude towards Gil.

As we pulled from the driveway onto the paved road, we passed Mattie and Theo in their pickup. They had taken a short trip into town this morning, and it didn't dawn on me until now that except for the folks at the cabins, Gil had been the only one around. The thought chilled me.

Brendan slowed down. "We're taking a drive through the park," he said through his open window. "We may be gone a while."

They waved and bid us a good time, Aunt Mattie promising she would stop by and take Pepper out. Then we were off, with me nearly bouncing off the seat.

"How long does it take to see the laurel?" I said tartly, piqued when my head almost bumped the roof.

"I thought maybe we'd make a day of it, have a picnic." He indicated a basket and small cooler behind the seats.

"If I'd known, I could've packed the lunch." I instantly regretted my snippy tone. My temper was without cause.

"It's really no problem," he said softly. "It'll be my treat this time. Don't worry, I'll let you reciprocate and keep your pride intact."

I deserved that, and though I could have stayed angry, what was the use? We weren't quarreling kids anymore, and there was no reason we couldn't be civil to each other. He was making half the effort. The least I could do was quit acting the bratty child.

"Sorry." I managed a smile and received his lazy grin in return.

"It's all right. No hard feelings, and if you'd rather not have the picnic, we can come back sooner."

"But I want to. Really. Where shall we stop?"

"I'll leave it up to you. When you see a spot you like, just holler. But first, we see the laurel."

As we drove into the mountains, my mood began to lift, and I felt better than I had since rising with the remnants of the strange dream upon me. When we began to climb higher, I left frustrations behind and found Brendan was right. It was a lovely day for a drive through the Smokies.

The morning sun had burned away all but a trace of the blue mists and every curve of the road brought into view a scene more splendid than the last. I remembered drives taken long ago with my father, times when we had made up stories about the fairies and elves who really did live in these enchanted mountains. They were treasured memories, moments stored away in my heart and not thought about for a long while…until seeing the rugged highlands again made me remember.

Brendan's question startled me out of my daydream.

"So, how many books have you had published?"

I slid him a sidelong glance. "Ten. Number eleven is in my computer."

"And they're mysteries?"

"For young adults, some with a touch of the supernatural. I've also had several novellas published in anthologies with other authors."

"Mattie tells me you won an award last year. Must be satisfying work."

"I suppose it's the same as any other job. Challenging, sometimes dreadful. But it's more than a job, it's who I am." Or at least who I had been up until three months ago.

"Did you always know you wanted to be a writer?"

I looked at him, where he sat so self-possessed behind the wheel. Even in his driving the man was easy-going, but was his interest in me genuine or just an attempt to make conversation?

"I remember having little notebooks, even when I was a kid, and making up stories. Maureen used to make fun of me, because I was always writing in my notebooks. Back then, Mother just thought me weird. I guess Daddy was the only one who really understood. I wonder now if he wasn't a closet writer himself." I considered the possibility for a moment before asking, "But what about you? Where have the years taken you?"

He tipped his head. "Hmm, where haven't they? To name a few places, Alaska, Vancouver, Wyoming, Montana. I've lived a lot of places west of Laurel Cove."

"I thought Aunt Mattie said you're a teacher."

"True, but only for the last two years. After high school, I joined up and did a stint in the army. I did some desert duty and then spent the rest of my time in Alaska. When I got out, I went after a biology degree. The day after I graduated, I got in my old pickup and started driving. For a year I worked long enough to get me from one place to the next and spent a lot of time backpacking the Rockies from Boulder to British Columbia. I lumberjacked in Oregon, hired on a highway crew in Wyoming."

This sounded more like the Brendan I remembered, and I couldn't help but wonder—why did he come back? He looked reflective when I asked.

"I guess you could say the vastness of the land got to be too much for me. I started to have a strange hankering for gentler mountains and quiet coves. Plus, my parents were having health problems and my sisters were still in college. I got my parents moved closer to Knoxville and my sisters graduated this past winter. So, my family is gone from here, but it's home to me."

I wondered if he was truly as contented as he sounded.

"You're here permanently then?"

He shrugged wide shoulders as he eased the vehicle around a bump in the road. "Nothing's permanent, is it? If I've learned anything in my life, it's to take things as they come. Ten years ago, I would never have believed I'd end up back in Laurel Cove, teaching a bunch of high school kids."

Silence fell between us, but it wasn't uncomfortable. I watched cloud shadows from above drift across clouds of a different kind. The edge of the road dropped away, sloping dizzily downward to a tiny valley sandwiched between two mountains. All across the valley and up the velvet slopes, laurel slicks bloomed in a burst of pink and white. It was heaven, or the closest thing to it, and I was still a part of it. The mountains, the laurel, the windswept heights and nestling valleys--they all gave me a sense of belonging, of finally coming home.

Later, while we picnicked by a mountain stream, I asked Brendan about the environmental group Mattie had mentioned. "Is it something you started?"

"You mean our Laurel Cove League?" He sounded almost self-conscious. "No, I didn't start it, but it's something I believe in very strongly. I couldn't help getting involved. It's just a local group, but we make ourselves heard. Folks often think just because there's a national park here in the Smokies, conservation is a sure thing. Actually, there is a lot to do toward protecting our cove."

"Such as?"

He threw me a quizzical glance, his brows knitting into a skeptical frown. "Do you really want to hear this?"

Now he thought I was just making small talk.

"Of course, I'm interested. I may have moved away, but I'm still concerned with anything that affects Laurel Cove."

I wasn't certain he believed this, but he went on.

"Making a long story short, a certain Harrison Enterprises wants to develop the land along the Lazy River in the Cove. They want to put in a big hotel, condos, golf course, and all sorts of garbage. They're trying to sell the idea to the Cove residents by telling them how many more job opportunities there would be, as well as places for their entertainment."

"Well, I suppose that would be true," I said, not expecting the explosion that followed.

"To hell with entertainment!" His hand smacked the picnic basket. "If folks want to be entertained, let them go to one of the towns near the park. They can find enough of it there."

I couldn't argue with him. The several towns nestled at the foot of Mt. LeConte, were lovely, but nonetheless they were places dedicated to tourism. Not a bad thing, but in the summer one could barely drive their narrow streets or stroll their sidewalks for the throngs of cars and people milling about. I remembered well and could easily understand his not wanting Laurel Cove to follow suit. But there was the advantage of new jobs the hotel would bring.

"How do people of the Cove feel about the idea?" I hoped he wouldn't erupt again.

I received a rueful look. "For the most part they're against it and content with the way things are. Oh, we like tourists and encourage them to stay in the Cove. After all, they are the ones who buy most of the local crafts like Theo's wind chimes and Mattie's quilts, but the kind of tourists we've always attracted are of a different sort. They're content to stay in small cabins and motels and even to camp. They don't need a huge concrete playground to keep them entertained. Laurel Cove has always been a community of farmers and artists and craftspeople. That's the way we want to keep it."

"You said for the most part everyone agrees. Do you mean there are some people who want the hotel?"

He set down the can of soda he'd been drinking from, and I saw his hand tighten around it, crinkling it slightly. "There are a few who would go along with it in a minute. The promise of big money in the Cove sounds good, and the whole idea is backed by somebody who talks smooth but has only mercenary in his heart."

"Anyone I know?" Who in the Cove was ready to cash in? Certainly not Mattie and Theo. They loved their little resort too much to want such stiff competition.

Brendan shook his red-brown head, and in spite of his full beard I saw a muscle twitch in his jaw.

"I won't mention any names of Cove people, but Deane Kimball, the editor of the *Pineville Gazette*, is all for it, and he has dedicated the last six months of his life to putting down the League every chance he gets. He runs at least one editorial a week tearing apart our quote, 'watchdog group.' Environmental crazies is another favorite term of his, among forest fanatics and ecology eccentrics. Neat little phrases, aren't they? Guaranteed to start folks wondering whose side we're really on."

"Sounds to me like he borders on yellow journalism. Not my idea of a good newspaper man."

He downed the last of his soda and stretched out on the blanket we'd spread on the ground. He sighed and clasped his hands behind his head. "Mine either. I can think of a way to shut him up. Trouble is, it would involve my landing in jail for assault, specifically for breaking his jaw and leaving him in need of a nose job."

"Brendan!" I couldn't help but gasp. The thought of physical violence of any sort sent chills running through me, and I suddenly found myself pulling my knees up and hugging them tightly. I had thought myself over these sudden flashbacks, but this one came out of the blue. I started shaking.

In an instant he sat up beside me, his hand resting gently on my arm. "What is it, Jane? This is the second time today you've gone funny on me. Is it something I said? I didn't mean to rant on. Please don't mind it."

"It's…not you…at all." I struggled to control my voice.

"Then what?"

Gazing into his turquoise eyes had a calming effect, and as my heart beat slower, I wondered if I dared to tell him the truth of my returning to the Cove. I didn't relish recanting the events of that night in my apartment, but at least then he would understand the reason for my sudden fear. And maybe, in talking it out, I would finally rid myself of the nightmare still hidden in my brain.

"How long?" he asked, when I'd finished telling him of the attack.

"It's been three months now. I suppose I should be over it. I know it's crazy to be so paranoid, but it's the simplest word, the smallest gesture brings it back, and I can't seem to control it. I don't know what to do to change—"

My voice broke and tears burned the back of my eyes. It would be so easy to give in and let the terror of that senseless attack control my life, but I had come this far and struggled so hard to put it behind me, it would be self-defeating to let this happen. Taking a deep breath, I forced myself to stop shaking.

Brendan seemed to understand my need for silence, and he said nothing for a few moments. Then he tipped his head sideways, as if listening for something.

"Can you hear it? Listen close."

I tilted my head too and caught the elusive sound. A soft musical roar, water spilling over rocks. "A waterfall?"

He grinned in answer. "You use to love them, didn't you? I remember you always talked about the fairies and elves you were certain lived behind them."

"And I probably wrote about them in a notebook somewhere. I suppose you think it's silly."

"What's so silly? I believe in them, or else who sneaks the money under your pillow when you lose a tooth?"

I found myself laughing at his mock chagrin and let him pull me to my feet. Yet I wasn't quite prepared when he continued to hold my hands and bending his head, brushed the corner of my lips with his own. The softness of his beard tickled my chin.

"What was that for?" I asked when he drew away.

"Let's just say for old time's sake and leave it at that. Come on, the falls aren't far up the trail."

The sun slanted through the thick canopy of spruce and fir and touched the tumbling stream of water, dancing across it and setting off small sparkling diamonds of light. We stood close enough to feel the fine spray of mist on our faces and smell the sweet mixture of laurel and pine. It was a rich, earthy scent and evoked many memories of happier times in the mountains.

I watched him touch a tiny cone from a nearby balsam. In maturity, it would turn purplish and stand straight on the conifer's boughs. It smelled pungent, and I secreted some of the scent away inside of me, to take out and enjoy when I returned to the city.

"It's a she-balsam," I said and pointed out the large rosin-filled blisters that grew on the trunks of perhaps half the trees around us. "The mountain people, when they found the clear liquid inside the blisters, compared it to mother's milk and called the tree a she-balsam. The red spruce doesn't have such blisters, and so they thought it to be the mate of the balsam, or he-balsam."

"You remember." He seemed surprised.

"There's a lot to remember about these mountains." I thought about the cabin in the woods and the story Aunt Mattie had told me. "Do you remember old Cissy Oliver? I walked by her cabin yesterday. Mattie says some people believe it's haunted now she's gone. I wonder if it is?"

"Ah yes, Cissy Oliver and the wild Sheridan O'Malley who loved her." Brendan smiled, but it was a thoughtful smile, and I didn't think he was making fun. "One of Laurel Cove's favorite legends. Too bad the old lady had to die the way she did."

Mattie hadn't told me about that, and suddenly I had to know. "How did she die?"

"Doctor said she was poisoned by one of her own herbs she grew in her garden. Seems strange after all those years. I mean, you think she would have known what was safe and what wasn't, but then she was pretty old. Could be she just made a mistake, or maybe…"

"Or maybe?"

He shrugged broad shoulders.

"She did it on purpose? Is that what some people think?"

"You know how people around here talk. Some said she was just tired of being alone, waiting to join Sheridan in the hereafter."

"So, she killed herself." The thought angered me, though I wasn't sure why. Except if Cissy had simply wanted to join Sheridan, wouldn't she have done it sooner? Why would she have waited so many years? "It doesn't make sense," I said. But then neither did my inexplicable desire to go closer to Cissy's cabin yesterday, nor the undeniable urge I felt to go there again.

I put aside the urge in order to enjoy the simple beauty of the falls and later, the more spectacular view from Clingman's Dome. Leaving the parking area below, we climbed the half-mile to the summit. The trail was paved, but it remained a steep steady ascent, and when we finally reached the top, I could only sink breathlessly down on the bench inside of the concrete tower.

The weekend crowd was a day away, and only a few early vacationers joined us in the observation tower. With a sigh, I gave myself up to the high altitude and the sheer beauty and mystery of the mountains. Brendan sat next to me, his arm brushing my shoulder, his rough hand seeking to close over mine. His nearness was comforting, and we sat in easy silence, watching the clouds rise and fall over the enchanted misty peaks.

"It's no wonder our ancestors settled here," he said softly. "The Stuarts and the McGarrens. Coming from Scotland the way they did, another land of hazy, rugged hills, it's no wonder they were drawn to the Smokies.

The mountains must have reminded them of home and yet gave them the freedom they craved. I've often wondered what they thought when they first saw these ridges."

I read a certain pensive quality in his rugged features, and I realized then just how much like the mountains he was—hard and raw as the loftier peaks, yet mysterious and compelling as the smoky-blue gentler ones.

"I imagine they felt much as we do now," I said, sharing an affinity with Brendan for those long-ago people who had traveled down the Appalachians until they came to this land. "I'm glad they did settle here. I can't imagine a more beautiful place to come home to."

The touch of his blue-green gaze settled on me. "Is that what you've done, Ceely Jane? Come home?"

In using the nickname, I thought he was asking more in his veiled question than I was willing to answer, and so I only said, "I suppose I have, at least for a little while."

He didn't press me further. We sat together a while longer, watching cloud shadows play on the mountains, enjoying the elusive sun, talking of inconsequential things that could only matter to two people who had grown up together. Somewhere in the afternoon, I began to forget about the brash youth Brendan had once been and began to be disturbed by the strange, enigmatic man he had become.

While we gazed out over the cloud-capped ridges, he asked me out the following night.

"You've a birthday to celebrate," His voice sounded awkward as he looked away. "We…could go to dinner in town."

"That would be nice, but how did you remember?"

When he looked at me, I saw a flicker of some nameless emotion in his eyes and his voice sounded hushed.

"There are some things you never forget. Even when you're a thousand miles away you remember the dogwood blooms in April and the mountain laurel in May. Some memories just never leave you, even if you sometimes wish they would."

Chapter 5

The sun remained just a dusky glow over the valley when we pulled up in front of Gran's house. Pepper met me at the door with a plaintive whine. I scooped her up and snuggled her in my arms.

"Poor baby," I crooned. "You hate being left alone in a strange place, don't you?"

"Why didn't the two of you just stay with Theo and Mattie?"

I didn't want to explain about my need to get over the fear of being alone. "I really have to decide what to do about Gran's house. I guess you know she left it to me, but it's been a year now. I can't let it sit empty forever."

Brendan put his hand on the door, preventing me from stepping inside. I glanced up at him curiously.

"You wouldn't ever consider selling out, would you?"

I didn't immediately follow his train of thought. Then suddenly, I knew what he meant. "You mean to Harrison Enterprises?" I shook my head. "No, never that."

"They might offer you a considerable sum of money. A part of your grandmother's property adjoins the river."

"I'm not interested in any sum of money." I searched his face, noting the frown wrinkling his brow. "Honest,

I'm not."

Pepper growled against my arm, and my skin prickled. Did she sense something here I didn't? Some undercurrent beneath Brendan's outward facade?

A rustle near the lilac bushes made me jump. A shadow emerged from near the end of the porch.

"Gil?" Brendan took a step backward and peered into the evening gloom. "Hey man, what're you doing here?"

Gil staggered closer, and I knew right away he'd been drinking.

"Hi ya, Brendan. I was just sittin' over by the flowers. Miz Althea used to sit there with me. She gave me lemonade sometimes."

Brendan stepped off the porch and went to put an arm around the unsteady Gil's shoulders. "You miss her, don't you, buddy?" he sympathized. "But I think you've been hitting something a little harder than lemonade. Not good for you, you know."

Gil grinned sheepishly. "Ah, I know, Brendan, but I get sad sometimes. It makes me feel better."

If I hadn't been so obsessed with my own fears, I might have felt sorry for Gil. Brendan certainly had no qualms about befriending him, but I couldn't shake my paranoia.

"You best be heading on home now, Gil. Theo will be looking for you to help him out tomorrow. You want a ride?"

Gil shook his head, rubbed his nose, and ran his hand through his greasy hair. "Nah, I'll be okay."

Brendan watched him stagger down the drive and disappear into the growing darkness. "Hope he makes it all right," I heard him murmur. "Sometimes I worry about the poor guy." He turned back to me, true concern darkening his eyes. "He lives by himself in his folks' old house now, and if Theo hadn't given him a job, he'd probably just wander around drunk all the time."

A sudden wave of compassion for the unfortunate Gil washed over me, but it mingled with quivers rippling down my backbone. I hugged Pepper close.

As if he sensed my distress, Brendan came back up on the porch.

"He's gone now, you don't have to worry." When I didn't answer, he dipped his head and looked into my face. "Hey, he really upset you, didn't he? Come on, let's go inside."

In the kitchen, he insisted I sit while he made coffee. Once I held a steaming mug in my hands, a calmness stole over me.

Leaning back against the counter, he looked down into his own cup. "Did you have a good time today?"

The coffee drove away the chill, and I remembered how wonderful I'd felt up at Clingman's Dome—refreshed, energized, washed clean. "Aside from the fact my feet hurt and I feel like I've been dragged up a mountain, it was nice." I managed a smile. "I realize I'm being silly about Gil. It's just I can't seem to get over this feeling of…of someone being after me."

"You don't have to explain. After my service in the desert, I saw plenty of people with PTSD." His eyes and voice were gentle and concerned. "Have you gone for some kind of counseling? You really should."

"It's mainly why I'm here. My therapist suggested I just get away for a while. I was certain the Cove and Gran's house would be a refuge."

"But fear likes to follow us wherever we go. And 'of

all base passions, fear is most accurs'd.'"

I glanced up, surprised at his quoting Shakespeare.

"Contrary to what you may have once believed, I was never exactly illiterate." His mouth lifted in a wry smile, but what emotion did I glimpse in his eyes? Something too brief to read and that bothered me. I didn't want to think it was only part of my trivial imaginings.

"I think it's time I go," he said and dumped the rest of his coffee in the sink. In walking past, his fingers touched my cheek for a fleeting moment and then he was gone.

Sleep had no sooner claimed me that night than a jumble of faces and figures assaulted my unconscious mind. At first none was familiar, then one emerged more vividly from the rest. The dark cloaked woman of the road. Once more she pleaded with me, begged me. The plaintive eyes pierced me while the tortured lips moved in some feverish request. She repeated something, but I couldn't tell what even though her beseeching mouth formed the request over and over again. Then, perversely, she was no longer the strange unknown woman but one who was familiar and beloved to me. Gran. It was Gran who called to me about something I must do. In confusion I reached for her, reached for the thin, crepe-papery hand she extended to me. I had to ask what she wanted because I needed to know what had been the last words she'd spoken to me.

But I wasn't to know yet. The dream ended with Gran disappearing into some endless void, and then I was awake, breathing hard and staring into the darkness of the room. When my heart finally returned to its normal beat, I pushed back the tangled sheets and sat up to run a shaking hand through my damp hair. Whatever had brought on this latest dream I didn't know, but it was certainly more disturbing than any of the others. It seemed so real, and even now, even while I sat here awake, it was as if I hadn't dreamt it at all but had really seen my grandmother's face.

I forced myself to try and sort it out rationally. Gran. Why was her memory bothering me? What was she trying to tell me in the dream? And the poor woman I'd seen on the road. Why had she returned to haunt me? *Who was she?*

Shivering, I shook away the mindless questioning. My nightshirt stuck to my clammy skin. Turning on the bedside lamp, I slid from the confusion of twisted sheets and hurried across the bare floor. I pulled a sweatshirt from the highboy and soon was snuggled in its fleecy warmth. Thank goodness I'd thought to bring it along. When I climbed back into the rumpled bed, Pepper eyed me grumpily. I wondered if she wasn't tired of my strange nighttime behavior, but as always, she was devoted to me. I took comfort from her small warm body curled at my feet.

It was all so ironic. I had come here to Laurel Cove to rest and recuperate from a terrifying experience, and all I'd succeeded in doing so far was to get more upset, first by some fanatic standing by the road, then by a drunken handyman, and now by this crazy nonsensical dream. And that's precisely what it was. A dream. I made up my mind to forget about it, forget about the strange lady, and refuse to let the sight of Gil Carson send shivers racing along my spine.

What was it my therapist said I should do? Oh yes, practice mindfulness. Focus on one word to alleviate the anxiety. Put everything else out of my mind and focus. I searched for a word and settled on laurel, hoping it would conjure up the sight of the pink and white blossoms. But try as I might, there was one thing I couldn't put from my mind so easily. The thought of Gran and of what she'd so desperately tried to tell me. What was it she had wanted me to know? Why had she told me, on her deathbed, there was a reason for me to come back to Laurel Cove? Why had she insisted my room be left untouched, and, not least of all, why had she returned to haunt my dream tonight?

* * *

While I dressed for dinner the next evening, I banished all thoughts of the dream from my mind. This was my thirtieth birthday, the big three-o, and I had every intention of enjoying it. After dinner, we were to stop in at the resort to share the lovely cake Mattie had already baked.

Not having brought a suitable dinner dress along, I'd spent the afternoon shopping in Pineville. My excursion into the single dress shop had produced a pale dusty rose affair with skinny straps and a short, flared skirt. Sitting at the cherry wood vanity now, I applied rose lipstick and picked at my hair. It was taking forever to grow out, but at least it no longer looked quite so spiky and stark.

I opened the small wooden jewelry box and exchanged tiny pearl earrings for thin gold hoops. Shutting the box, I rested my hand on the intricately engraved top with its laurel blossoms. It had once belonged to Gran, and she had given it to me many years ago.

Before Brendan arrived, Mattie came over.

"You look just lovely, honey." She hugged me close

then stepped back, her eyes suddenly misting. "You are certainly not the little Janey-girl I used to know."

I glanced away, knowing it wouldn't take much for my own eyes to tear up. "Do you suppose the air-conditioning will be cool in the restaurant? Maybe I should take a sweater." While I thought nothing of wearing dresses like this to a cocktail party in New York, a self-conscious doubt about wearing it tonight teased me. "Maybe I should change into something else."

Aunt Mattie patted my shoulder. "You never mind, Janey-girl. But look here, so you don't turn Brendan's head too much, I have just the thing for you to wear." I noticed she carried folded over her arm some silky fringed fabric, ivory in color.

"This ought to compliment your pretty dress really fine." She unfolded the fabric and draped it softly over my shoulders. A lovely, delicately embroidered shawl now covered the bareness of the dress.

"It's beautiful, Aunt Mattie," I murmured and admired the pale dusty roses stitched flat along the edge of the shawl. From them hung long fluid strands of fringe. I knew the shawl must be quite old.

"It was your Gran's," Mattie said wistfully and stood back to view me in it. "Your grandpa bought it for her when he was stationed overseas, and she always treasured it. I just know she'd want you to have it. Looks much better gracing your slender shoulders than it ever did mine. I've never had the figure to go with such a delicate thing as it."

I kissed her cheek. "I'll wear it tonight, proudly and with much pleasure."

We hugged and then Mattie set me away from her, a gleam of amusement shining in her eyes. "Whatever perfume you're wearing, you best take care. It just may go to Brendan's red head."

I had the distinct feeling she hoped it might.

When Brendan arrived, I couldn't help noticing how very different he looked dressed in neatly pressed khaki pants, pale blue shirt and summer brown sports jacket. I'd never seen him dressed in anything other than faded jeans and rumpled shirts. Even his hair and beard appeared to have been trimmed, and I found myself thinking what a truly handsome man he was.

Visitors crowded the town, as always, but we dined in a restaurant located at the edge of the mass of shops, hotels and tourist traps that lined the main street. The food was delicious and we both relaxed with talk coming easily between us. At least while I was with Brendan, all thoughts of strange dreams faded away.

After dinner we strolled through the streets, wandering past darkened curio shops and art galleries, pausing to look in windows at the local crafts they displayed. Above the crowded streets, Mt. LeConte loomed dark and intriguing in the twilight. The mountains could certainly weave their magic about you, but then the entire evening had a magical quality to it, as if for the first time in many weeks peace had settled in my soul.

The harmony lingered on the drive home, and the sweetness of the Tennessee night lulled me into further complacency. It wasn't until we entered the Cove that a vague sense of uneasiness returned, and while rounding a curve in the winding road I felt it, like a shock of static electricity. As if suddenly commanded to do so, I sat bolt upright and stared straight ahead.

"What is it?" Brendan asked. "Or were you just

falling asleep?"

Had I been and already starting to dream? Or had I really seen someone back there, standing alongside the road? Someone who seemed small and dark-robed and beckoning? If I had, then so surely had Brendan. I glanced at him.

"Was there anyone walking along the road?" I turned to glance behind us but saw nothing.

"Not that I noticed."

"Then I must have just imagined it." I was only half-convinced.

"Maybe a little too much champagne?" But he must have seen me shiver. Reaching behind him he produced a flannel shirt and bade me to slide it around my shoulders. I didn't argue but covered the shawl and the flimsy dress with it. Perhaps it was the woodsy scent of the flannel that eased the sudden unrest, but for a moment I was safe again.

When we stopped in front of the house, I was reluctant to get out, as if I knew what awaited me, another night of strange dreams. In spite of the nightmare I had experienced in the city, I almost wished I was back in my apartment. Almost, but not quite.

"What is it, Jane? You're spooked again, and Gil's not even around."

"It's nothing," I brushed away the senseless disquiet. "And I forgot, we're supposed to go to Aunt Mattie's for cake, and I need to pick up my dog." Relief that, for at least a short time, I'd won a reprieve from going into the house alone, settled on me.

Brendan joined us for a simple celebration in the sunporch. Mattie and Theo presented me with one of my uncle's hand-carved wind chimes that looked like a flock of birds poised in flight.

"Thank you both, so much." I kissed them each on the cheek and promised the wind chimes would find a special place in my apartment.

"Not many places where the wind blows through, I'm sure." Theo stroked his mustache thoughtfully. "But maybe when you look at it, it will remind you of the mountains…and of us."

Later, Brendan walked me to the front door of the farmhouse. I let Pepper in ahead of me and turned to say goodbye, but he hesitated a moment, then slipped a small slender box from his pocket.

"I'm sorry this isn't wrapped. There was something I needed to add at the last minute. I…hope you'll like it."

The usually confident and brash Brendan seemed suddenly uncertain, as if worried I wouldn't like his gift.

The gold chain and locket were exquisite and I hesitated accepting something so expensive, but had I refused, he would certainly have taken it the wrong way. Lifting it from the box, I held it gently in my hand.

"It's beautiful," I whispered, touched by the sweetness of his gesture.

"Look inside."

Nestled in the cradle of the locket lay an infinitely tiny pink porcelain laurel blossom. With a catch in my throat, I thought of how it represented the mountains and the place of my birth.

And then I thought again of the story Aunt Mattie had told me, about Cissy and Sheridan O'Malley and of how they'd found him with a cluster of laurel blossoms upon his chest, covering the bullet hole. Had Cissy put it there? This many years later it shouldn't matter, but somehow it did…to me.

I couldn't express any of this to Brendan, but I thanked him and let him fasten the locket about my neck. And when he turned me about and tipped my face up to his, I accepted his kiss. Warm and sensuous, his lips melded against mine, igniting a slow fire I believe surprised us both. The shawl slipped from my shoulders. Brendan's hands slid down my bare arms, and then he drew me closer until I could feel his chest rising and falling rapidly against my own. I sensed he was holding himself back, but the more startling revelation was I didn't want him to. More than anything I wanted to lose myself in this man, to hold onto his strength and let him keep the nightmares at bay.

But it was not yet to be. As if sensing my mindless surrender, Brendan lifted his mouth from mine and took a step back, though his hands still clasped my arms.

I looked up into his face and saw passion had darkened his eyes to a smoky hue. "You need to go in," he said huskily. "I'll…see you tomorrow."

I didn't remember having made plans to see him the next day, but I gave no argument. And all night long, I wore the locket he had given me and let the warm memory of his kiss keep away my fears.

* * *

When Brendan did stop by the following afternoon, he found me immersed in getting the teen-age hero of my book out of a particular jam.

"Am I interrupting something important?" Dressed once more in jeans and a faded work shirt, he lounged against the porch railing not far from where I had curled into a wicker chair, laptop propped on my knees. "I didn't realize this was a working vacation for you."

"I really need to get back into the swing of things

again and finish this book. It…hasn't been easy these past weeks."

He nodded in understanding, then shrugged. "I'll leave you to your work this morning, but I have an idea for this afternoon, if you're game."

"Idea?"

"Friend of mine runs a small riding stable in the Cove. You used to be a regular Annie Oakley. How about going for a trail ride up in the hills?"

The truth was, I hadn't been riding in years. Common sense told me I should bow out and stick to the writing, but common sense didn't seem very appealing at the moment. After a brief hesitation, I said, "Only if you'll promise to take it slow and easy."

Our eyes locked for an instant, and I think we both knew I wasn't speaking of just the riding.

Later, while Brendan waited on the porch, I went inside and changed into jeans and a cotton shirt. I took my camera along, slipping the strap over my head, and went to look for Pepper. I found her dozing under the lilac bushes. This time, I would drop her by the resort, where I knew she'd feel more secure in my absence.

The riding stable occupied what had once been one of the larger farms of the Cove. The farmer, Brendan told me, had some years ago decided it was time to retire. None of his children was interested in running the farm, and so he sold it, but not to someone with big development ideas.

"Chet's a pretty good guy. He's real supportive of the League. He figures the sort of tourists who frequent a hotel complex would be more interested in playing golf than riding horses."

It made sense, yet when I met Chet a few minutes

later, I had to wonder how much longer he could continue in his work. Like Theo and Mattie, he was not young. Wispy hair streaked with various shades of gray peaked out from beneath his straw cowboy hat, and the gnarled hands that led the horses out and readied them for us were not as steady as they'd probably been when he'd opened the stable years ago.

"You ridden much?" was all he said when he handed over the reins to me.

"My sister and I rode ponies when we were kids, but that was a while ago. Brendan's promised no galloping today."

Chet graciously helped me up into the saddle and told me the few words I needed to know to make the little bay gelding behave.

"He's part Arab and he can be feisty, but just let him know who's boss and he'll settle right down. Now, you keep an eye on her, Brendan."

We started off, Brendan astride McTavish, a tall red roan, and myself finding Staccato a pleasure to ride, as if he knew I needed him to be a gentleman today.

The morning turned out to be a pure joy. We rode side by side and took turns pointing out various sights of interest, reining the horses in long enough to view the valley from atop a surrounding foothill.

The Cove lay spread out before us like some agrarian paradise. I busied myself taking a dozen pictures before Brendan threatened to leave me to my own devices. Along an old mountain trail, we dismounted and rested a while among delicate violets and pale mauve rhododendron. The rich earthy smell of the woods was intoxicating. Laurel bloomed freely here, a sweet evanescent fragrance, and he plucked a small cluster and tucked it behind my ear, his fingers resting gently against my cheek before he turned to the horses again.

Was he thinking of the kiss we'd shared last night? What had it meant to him? Had I been anything like my friends back in New York, I would've come right out and asked, but I'd never been bold in any aspect of my life, least of all love. The last serious relationship I'd had a few years ago had ended on a sour note, and I'd been wary of trusting anyone since. Maybe, as Maureen sometimes said, I needed to be more aggressive; but aggression was distasteful to me. I was more inclined to just let Fate have its way, especially where Brendan was concerned.

On the way back, we rode along the Lazy River and cut down the dirt two-track that led to Gran's, now my, property. With the tall trees around us, I let my thoughts wander.

"It's been over a year, but it's strange to think of Gran's place as mine, and I'm still not sure why she left it all to me. Why not leave it to Theo and Mattie, as she did the resort? Anyway, I've been thinking maybe it's what I should do. Sign the place over to them. It adjoins the resort. They could even expand, put up a few more cabins, or move into the farmhouse and rent out their bungalow."

"I think Theo and Mattie have all they can do to run the resort. They're not so young anymore."

I leaned forward to brush a fly off Staccato's neck. "So they've already informed me, but what will I do with the house and property? It seems foolish for it to sit empty except when I'm here, and how often would it be? I only plan to stay a few weeks now."

McTavish moved closer alongside me, Brendan's leg brushing against mine. "Your grandmother left you her house for a reason, I think. She knew there might come a time when you needed a place to come to, somewhere you'd feel safe."

Maybe that was true, except I hadn't really felt so safe since coming back to the Cove. Strange things had happened, the black-robed woman on the road, the lure of the cabin in the woods, the unreasonable fear of Gil…and the dreams. Even now, like the terror that had brought me back to the Cove in the first place, they came back to haunt me. Children's voices chanting. Bewildered eyes searching mine. Gran's hand reaching out.

"What is it?" his voice cut through to me.

I realized I'd pulled Staccato up short in the middle of the road. The gelding shook his head, bridle jangling as he protested my sudden decision. Obviously, he only wanted to return to the stable.

I glanced up into the woods, staring once more into vacant windows. The eyes and soul of a house no longer inhabited, at least not by anyone of this world. Voices whirled about in my mind. *Lights have been seen in the cabin, after dark. Some say she doesn't rest at all, but walks at night.* Then, from somewhere, the echo of a dog's plaintive howl sent icy fingers sliding down my backbone.

"I was here the other day," I said, my voice hushed. "I didn't know it was Cissy's cabin, but now I remember being here a long time ago, when the other kids were taunting her. It was awful, and I knew Gran would be upset with me. I think maybe she felt sorry for Cissy, or maybe she even knew her, before it happened."

"Before what happened?" Brendan drew next to me and leaned over to put his hand on mine where I gripped the reins.

I tore my gaze from the cabin and looked into his turquoise eyes. "The murder."

He considered this a moment before he said, "I think we should leave now."

Did he feel it too? The presence of someone other than us?

We did not talk at all as we rode away, but I couldn't resist a single backward glance at the lonely cabin. Strange how the breeze sifting through the trees now sounded more like someone's gentle sighing. *Cecilia Jane.*

Chapter 6

I set up the laptop at the kitchen table the next day and prepared to struggle with my sixteen-year-old hero once more. But time and again my mind wandered and I found myself jumping up, to pour more iced tea, to turn my fan up a click. The day grew warmer, the humidity rising along with the temperature. Finally, I saved everything and snapped the laptop shut. Snatching my camera and a small notebook, I went out to wander around the yard, poking at the fading lilacs and watching a hummingbird hover at the morning glories.

Pepper lazed on the porch and had no interest in joining my aimless steps. I didn't bother to cajole her. Without really thinking about it, I began to wander behind the house, through the field of wildflowers growing in such colorful profusion. Halfway across the back of the property, I met with Gil.

"Hi there, Miz Jane. Where y'all headed?" He nodded politely, and I knew I had to at least try and be friendly.

"Just taking a walk. No place in particular."

"Thought maybe you'd be tired out, after goin' ridin' and all." He fell in step beside me as I kept walking. "Brendan's a nice fella, ain't he? He's always real nice to me. Is he your boyfriend?"

The question stopped me, and I glanced at Gil, realizing then just how truly simple—and innocent—he was.

"No, not really," I tried to explain. "We sort of grew up together. We've known each other a long time."

"But he likes you real well. I can tell. You looked real pretty when you went with him, in your fancy dress."

To think Gil had noticed me in the slinky dress made me nervous. He might be simple, but he was still a man. "Th-thank you." I thought quickly and pretended to be looking toward Aunt Mattie's house. "I think I see Uncle Theo over there. I bet he's looking for you, Gil."

I was lucky I could divert his attention so easily. In a moment, he ambled off toward the resort. Guilt at deceiving him plagued me, but the relief at not having him dogging my steps was greater. Especially since my steps were drawn to the woods again. The lure of tall trees and rushing river proved too much, and I soon found myself shut off from the sun.

I really did mean to go to the river, to only stop along the way to photograph hidden wildflowers. I had no conscious intention of going closer to the cabin. But when it came into view, I suddenly knew what I had to do. Like the hummingbird drawn to the morning glories, I was drawn to the forlorn little cabin that had been Cissy Oliver's home. Home? More like her prison.

I walked down the narrow path and stepped onto the sloping stoop, the rotting boards creaking beneath my feet. Did I dare look inside? Curtains darkened the two narrow windows facing the front, but strangely enough the door hung open an inch or so. Without a second thought, I gave it a gentle push. It groaned but swung wide, as if inviting me inside. A draft of cool air rushed out and for one instant I shrank back. Then, as if someone guided me, I stepped through the doorway.

I let my eyes adjust to the dimness before venturing further inside. The single room combined kitchen and sitting room. A field stone fireplace took up one wall, but there was nothing grand about it. It was strictly a necessity, the only source of heat when winter winds blew across the mountains, blanketing the Cove with snow.

What drew me closer into the room, reached out and touched me in some poignant way, was the small armless rocker that sat alone in front of the cold hearth. When I lay my hand along the back of the chair, it moved slightly, and I imagined for a moment Cissy sitting, rocking silently in her solitude.

I glanced around and noticed the bunches of dried herbs hanging here and there, the clay pots holding now shriveled plants. On a table in the corner sat a crude wooden mortar and pestle, and on shelves above it, earthenware jars. It looked as though Cissy had been quite the herbalist, and I remembered again the title the children of the Cove had given her—Witch Cissy.

I might have been satisfied to leave then, but a soft sound, I was never sure what, drew me to another room in the back of the cabin. Within it a single narrow bed stood against one wall, so different from my own cuddly four-poster. Beside it sat a tall chest of fine cherry wood, and above it hung a small round mirror. I went to peer into it.

It was cloudy with dust and age, but suddenly I had a vision in my mind of another woman standing in this same spot, brushing her fair-gold hair before it had turned to silver, biting her lips to make them pink, pinching her cheeks to make them blush, awaiting the arrival of Sheridan O'Malley.

Perhaps she had stood here that very night, had made herself pretty for him, and waited...and waited...only to be told by the sheriff from Pineville that the wild Irishman would never swagger through her door again.

Why had she not told the truth then? Why didn't she speak up and declare her innocence? Surely people of the Cove would have believed their schoolteacher. Surely, they would not have condemned her to a life surrounded by taunts and lies. Why had she let them believe until the day she died that she had indeed been the one to cut down Sheridan O'Malley?

If only there was some way of knowing the truth. Could the truth maybe even be found somewhere in this cabin?

The question taunted me as the children's song had once taunted Cissy. I looked around the cell-like room, my gaze resting on the narrow chest. Made of deep red cherry wood, it was a fine piece of furniture. Too bad it remained here, empty and unappreciated.

Or was it empty? Had anyone ventured in after Cissy's death to remove her belongings? The rest of the cabin looked undisturbed. Did I have the right to look into the chest?

Setting my camera down, I gave the glass knobs a tentative pull. The drawer yielded to display only a folded nightgown of white cotton and an assortment of plain handkerchiefs of the same. I tried each drawer and found nothing more than a set of muslin sheets, their creased edges frayed, and a few simple towels. Cissy had worn only those long dark dresses, had apparently never again felt the desire or need to look pretty after Sheridan was gone.

One drawer left and I figured it was all for naught. It creaked and resisted and appeared to be empty. I almost pushed it shut, then I saw it. The folded newspaper or at least the front page of one. Brittle and yellowed with age, the edges of it crumbled a bit when I picked it up. Fearing it might fall to pieces in my hand, I lifted it carefully, pushed the drawer shut with my knee and carried my discovery into the main room.

I sat in the armless rocker, gently spreading the paper open on my lap. The newsprint was faded and the picture blurred, but I had no trouble making out the face, the small mouth, the too-large eyes, the volume of light-colored hair. Even if the headline spilled across the top of the page hadn't told me, I would have known. This was Cissy. This was the paper telling of the murder. This was the way she had looked the day the sheriff had taken her in for questioning. Below her picture was another, this of a handsome, rakish sort of fellow with dark hair and laughing eyes. Sheridan. The wild Irishman, who after that fateful night had laughed no more.

They must have made an attractive couple; Cissy with her wispy fairness, he with such roguish good looks. I forced down a sudden lump in my throat. Were they finally together? Or was it true what some folks said, that Cissy did not rest?

The cabin grew darker, and I could not make out the faded words. I decided to take the paper with me, back to the house, where I could peruse it in the light. But I didn't want anyone to know about my discovery. Aunt Mattie and Uncle Theo would be upset to know I'd been here. Yet I was reluctant to leave. I leaned back in the rocker and slowly pushed it back and forth.

When did I first notice it? The sudden waft of cool

air that stirred the dust on the hearth, and changed the scent in the cabin from dusty dried herbs to light mountain fragrance? Laurel. Unmistakably, the scent of mountain laurel filled the room.

She was here. It was true what folks said. Cissy didn't rest. She roamed her cabin…searching for someone, something to set her spirit free. I wasn't afraid but a strong poignant sadness filled me, as if I could truly feel the way Cissy had while she lived here alone.

How much time passed? I couldn't be sure, but I knew when she left. Once more the cabin smelled of dried herbs and dust. Tucking the paper safely against me, I left the cabin and hurried back down the shadowy path.

I waited until evening, when I'd settled onto the sofa, to study the newspaper page. For the first time I noticed the date. In three days, it would be exactly sixty-five years since the Pineville Gazette had printed the story of Sheridan O'Malley's death. In all probability, it had only been a weekly paper at the time, but there was a chance that thirty-five years before the day I was born, someone had pulled a gun and shot Sheridan…and let Cissy take the blame. I don't know why, but I was certain of her innocence. More certain than I'd been of anything in my life. Cissy Oliver had not killed the man she loved.

I read the article painstakingly but gleaned only one fact Aunt Mattie had not already told me. Cissy had only been a nickname of the young teacher. Her given name? Cecilia.

I closed my eyes against this discovery. It seemed incredulous, yet how much was coincidence and how much intentional? Quite possibly I had been born on the anniversary of the murder. We shared the same name.

Had someone in my family suggest I be named after Cissy? If so, it was an unfunny joke. If not, then there was something more at work here than anyone had ever suspected.

Thankfully, I did not dream that night and sat eating breakfast the next morning when Brendan stopped by to ask if I would like to attend a meeting of the Laurel Cove League in the evening.

"We're going to come up with some firm plans to thwart Harrison Enterprises. If we don't move fast, they'll be in here bulldozing before we know it."

He leaned against the counter and helped himself to a blueberry muffin I'd made. I couldn't help but notice the way the morning sun shone off his hair again, the way his hands moved so sure and able. Then I remembered how his hands had slipped down my arms, how his lips had pressed against mine…

"Hey, are you there?" He sat down across from me and took my hand that lay palm up on the table. "What is it? You look a little spacey."

Too embarrassed to tell him the truth, I just shrugged and let my hand curl into the warmth of his. Would going with him tonight push me closer to something I wasn't yet ready to handle? Perhaps, but I said I would attend the meeting with him.

Later, I waited for him on the porch. When his vehicle turned into the drive, my heart gave a lurch, and I knew I probably was letting myself in for trouble where my heart was concerned. Just being with Brendan these past few days had certainly helped me start to forget my reason for coming back to the Cove.

The League met at the small community library that

served the Cove's population. Aside from a galley kitchen in the back, the building consisted of one room, and folks crowded in tonight. Some stood in little clusters, others sat at folding tables and chairs, all talked quietly but intently to one another. Even Aunt Mattie and Uncle Theo had decided to come tonight. They sat with Jed Hamilton. Aunt Mattie waved to me, but I didn't try to make my way over to her.

When Brendan walked to the podium at the front of the room, young and old turned their attention to him. I slid into an empty chair near the back.

I saw another side of Brendan during the meeting, a man commanding and in authority yet respected by the others gathered here. Everyone listened politely as he talked about Harrison Enterprises and the hotel complex and condos they proposed to build in Laurel Cove. Discussion quickly followed, and it was evident the folks here were all most definitely opposed to the venture. I recalled how vehement Brendan himself had become while talking about the project to me, yet now he remained calm, even when an attractive young woman jumped up and suggested they form an organized protest outside the city hall in Pineville.

"Just like Brendan said, we need to get vocal about this and we need to do it fast. If we don't, there are going to be construction workers crawling all over the Cove."

She seemed most adamant in her belief and I had to admire her commitment, but I couldn't help notice the intense gaze she kept fastened on Brendan, how she hung on his every word. *Perhaps it's Brendan himself she's committed to.* She might be a little young for him, third year of college maybe, but a curvy figure and wealth of auburn hair made her very attractive. I suddenly had a wild thought—of what striking children they would have, all red-haired with searing blue-green eyes.

I soon learned Stefanie belonged to a group of fifteen college students doing a summer seminar in the Cove. They'd become interested in the League's battle and were eager to offer whatever help they could.

"We'd be glad to organize the protest," one of the young men offered. "We staged a sit-in on campus last year to draw attention to the food served in the cafeteria. Too much fat and cholesterol, you know. They finally put in a salad bar."

I had to hide a smile, wondering if the two causes were equal in this fellow's mind.

"Thanks, Jeff," Brendan said. "Talk to me after the meeting, and we'll see what we can set up. I hate to see it come to this, but if Harrison offers someone enough money to sell out, well, we all know money talks. We need to make everyone in the Cove aware of how this complex would change their lives forever."

"How about we set up a social media blitz? And bombard the *Gazette* with letters to the editor?"

"There's a town meeting in Pineville next week. We should all attend."

The ideas went on and on as one hour turned into two. My brain began to weary of taking it all in, and I slipped into an old habit of observing people's facial expressions and trying to guess what they were thinking. Most everyone here was an open book tonight...except for two men who sat quietly, offering no comments. One was Jed Hamilton. He sat beside Theo with his arms folded across his narrow chest, his brows drawn together in a deep frown beneath the brim of his cap. I couldn't tell if the frown was because he agreed with the group or thought them wrong. The other man was probably about Brendan's age, of average height with very dark hair and thick glasses. Not really handsome, yet compelling in an intellectual sort of way. His expression remained totally impassive, his face devoid of any emotion.

I sighed with relief when Brendan called the meeting to a close. As the group slowly filed out of the library, I inched my way over to Mattie and Theo.

"Well, how about it, Uncle Theo. Are you ready to be part of a sit-in?"

He only shook his head sadly. "Too bad it's come to this. Wish those big fellows would go elsewhere with their hotels and condos."

"Mattie tells me you're staying at the farmhouse," Jed said to me. "Have you decided yet whether you'll sell it?"

"I haven't really thought about it," I hedged. "It's not an easy decision to make."

"I'm sure it isn't. Your family has been part of this Cove for more than a hundred years. Your grandparents were well respected by everyone. It would be a shame to see the old house torn down."

I wondered if this meant he too was against Harrison Enterprises.

In a friendly gesture, he put one hand on Uncle Theo's shoulder. "I guess being a good neighbor sort of runs in your family. Look how Theo and Mattie have given Gil a chance to prove himself."

"Well, if there's one thing everyone deserves it's a chance," Aunt Mattie spoke one of her favorite adages.

"That's what his folks told me before they passed on. They hoped the Cove would give Gil a chance. I tried to have him work in my hardware but unfortunately, he couldn't quite cope with the customers. Working with you, Theo, is probably the best thing for the poor fellow."

Before leaving, Jed drew Uncle Theo aside. The two talked quietly for several minutes.

Watching them, Aunt Mattie seemed nervous. I started to ask if everything was all right, but then Brendan came up beside me and leaned close to my ear.

"I really didn't expect things to drag on this long. I'm sure you're ready to leave."

Truth be told, I was more than ready to escape the stuffiness of the crowded room, but I didn't like my aunt's worried frown. Mattie simply never frowned. A moment later, Jed Hamilton left and Theo and Mattie followed close behind. When the library finally cleared, Brendan and I stepped out into the warm Tennessee night.

Before we climbed into the four-wheel drive, someone from the college group called out.

"We're all headed over to Shirley's Diner. You'll come, won't you? Your friend is welcome, too." I realized it was Stefanie talking, her head stuck out the window of Jeff's ancient van.

Brendan gave me a questioning look. I shrugged.

"After all this, I could do with something cold to drink. We won't stay long," he promised.

Shirley's Diner, on the highway to Pineville, boasted tables with red and white checkered clothes and Alan Jackson playing on the jukebox. When we joined the group of young people, Stefanie quickly motioned for Brendan to sit beside her. When he pulled two chairs out on the opposite side of the table, I didn't miss for a minute the challenge in her green eyes.

Seated with the boisterous college group, I felt like

a housemother on an outing with her charges. They ordered nachos and pitchers of soda and continued to hatch up ideas for thwarting Harrison Enterprises. They only stopped talking when the food arrived.

I was helping myself to the nachos when I recognized a man walking into the diner. He'd been at the meeting, the man with glasses. He'd shed his suit jacket and loosened his tie, and so looked much less sophisticated. When he spotted us, he grinned and strolled over to our table.

"So, the subversives are at it." His gaze slid around the group and settled on Brendan. From the way the two glared at each other, I could tell there was no love lost here.

"What do you want, Deane?" Brendan muttered.

"Only a piece of Shirley's coconut cream pie. Any objections?"

If looks could have killed, the group would have done away with the man right then. This had to be Deane Kimball, editor of the *Pineville Gazette*.

"You've got a lot of nerve even talking to us after the lousy editorials you did," Stefanie spoke up. "*Forest fanatics, environmental crazies*. How could you stoop so low?"

He smirked, then noticed me staring at him. An interested light suddenly shone in his eyes. He moved closer and introduced himself. "I don't believe we've met. Are you new to the Cove? College teacher working over the summer here?"

I sensed Brendan's tensing beside me, and I shivered a little when everyone's gaze fastened on me.

"Actually, I spent a lot of growing-up years in the Cove. My grandmother died last year, and I've just come back to stay in her house for a while."

"To think about selling it, no doubt. Now is certainly the time. Unless you've let yourself be influenced by this group."

"Not that it's any of your business, Deane," Brendan growled, "but Jane has no intention of selling out to Harrison."

"Just offering some friendly advice. I understand Harrison has already approached certain Cove residents, but I'm sure they'd rather deal with someone eager to sell."

"That wouldn't be me," I said, irritated that everyone seemed to think it's what I'd come down here to do. "It's not what my grandmother would want."

For a split second, Deane Kimball almost looked thoughtful, then tugging his tie a bit looser he headed for the counter.

The conversation at our table faded after that, and once the food was gone and the bill paid the students drifted out to their cars.

"We'll work on the letter campaign to the paper," Jeff promised Brendan. "It'll really annoy Kimball, I'm sure, and if there's anything else we can do, let us know."

Preoccupied, Brendan nodded. Suddenly, he had to sidestep Stefanie who'd planted herself in front of him. Thumbs hooked in the pockets of her hip-hugging jeans, auburn hair bouncing around her shoulders, she looked quite the impish charmer.

"I'd help Jeff get those letters out and some social media blasts, too, but my laptop has been acting wonky."

I watched his reaction. Was the smile he gave Stefanie one of kind indulgence…or something more?

"I'll be at the high school tomorrow. Stop by and you

can use my computer. Thanks for coming to the meeting tonight."

I knew she stood in the parking lot watching us climb into the four-wheel drive before heading off to Jeff's van. It made me more than a bit uncomfortable to feel her staring after us.

Was Brendan really oblivious to her true motives, or was he playing the game, too? It was difficult to say for certain, and why should it matter to me anyway? I had no claim on him, yet in just a few days' time, I had come to draw on his strength, to feel things I had no right to feel. Determinedly, I kept my silence and stared out into the night, a night with no moon and few stars.

Several miles down the highway, Brendan broke the silence. "You need to know Deane can be quite the charmer when he sets out to interest a woman."

The statement jolted me. "Why should that concern me?"

"He's been known to pick up on when someone is vulnerable."

"And you think I am."

He took the turn into the Cove a little too fast. I clutched at the seat to keep my balance. On both sides of the road, solid oaks rose up, dark silhouettes against an even darker sky.

"Face it, Jane. You've been through a lot lately. The attack, coming down here, staying in your grandmother's house again…without her, deciding what to do about it."

"That's it, isn't it?" I snapped. "That's what you're really worried about. It isn't concern for me. It's wondering what I'll do with Gran's house. Wondering if I'll give in after all and sell out to the highest bidder."

His hands tightened on the wheel, and he thrust his

jaw forward. "You know that's not true," he said very quietly.

"No, I don't. Any more than I know if it's right to try and keep progress from coming to the Cove. Maybe folks here deserve a chance to better themselves. Maybe welcoming Harrison Enterprises is the key to the success that's always eluded Laurel Cove. You can't judge what's good for everybody by what's good for you, Brendan."

For once, he didn't have a speedy comeback and silently I upbraided myself for being so outspoken. Yet it needed to be said. In some ways, he was as stiff-necked as Deane Kimball.

I stared out the window at the passing shadowy woods. Maybe coming back to Laurel Cove had been one big mistake. Maybe I should just pack up and go home, the sooner the better. I very nearly said so, but my throat closed up on the words.

She was there again. Walking along the road, her long black robe trailing about her ankles, her face hidden in the voluminous folds of the hood. Dressed so, she barely stood out against the moonless night, but I saw her, plain as if the sun had been shining at high noon. I waited for Brendan to say something, to acknowledge he'd seen her. When he didn't, a cold wave washed over me, setting my skin to tingling. I wrapped my arms around myself and struggled to stay in control.

A mile farther and I finally dared to speak. "That was odd."

He glanced at me. "What?"

"You...didn't see?"

"See what? What on earth are you talking about?"

I had seen her. *I had!*

There was another road to the river, and it

intersected with the one behind Gran's house. I grabbed Brendan's arm and pointed to it.

"Turn here. Please." My voice rose barely above a whisper. He gave me a baffled look but did as I requested.

"I hope you're going to tell me what this is all about," he said, cutting down the dirt two track leading into the woods. "I'd like to think maybe parking by the river in the moonlight is what you have in mind, but since there's no moon, I doubt it."

I only shook my head for an answer. When we came up to the spot, I just said, "Stop here."

When he realized where we were, Brendan observed me with quiet exasperation.

"So, this is it. Dear Jane, I think you've become obsessed."

Obsessed? Perhaps a better word might be possessed. After seeing the strange lady on the road again, I wondered. And now here I was straining to see through the woods, hoping to catch a glimpse of dancing, wavering lights in an empty cabin.

At my urging, he cut the engine and for a time we sat, not speaking, barely breathing, just watching. Through the open windows I smelled the softness of the languid summer night, heard the hypnotic whir of buzzing insects, and began to feel almost mesmerized by the subtle song of the woods. Yet still I watched, wanting only to see with my own eyes a sign that the spirit of Laurel Cove was here, that she did not rest.

Finally, Brendan said, "There's nothing here." He drove on down to where the road dead-ended at the river. As he turned the vehicle around, I watched the river. It looked so different by night, shimmering like black satin even in the darkness, satin that flowed on and on, while in the woods the little people played, perhaps oblivious to us mortals and our whims.

Was this whole place enchanted? Haunted? How did one cope with the feeling of being touched by something unknown?

Once back on the main road, he sighed. "What is it? What's the connection with you and the old cabin?"

I wanted to tell him—about the dreams, the woman I'd seen, the paper I'd found in Cissy Oliver's cabin. Somehow, they were all connected...and they all were tied to me. But how did I even begin to explain it to him without sounding like I'd completely lost my mind?

I left the question hanging, and when we reached the farmhouse, I bade Brendan a quick goodnight.

Chapter 7

I didn't have to wait long for an answer. The dreams assaulted me even before I fully slept. Unlike the previous night, they were vividly real. First the figure of Gran appeared as she'd looked the last time I saw her, her body pitifully frail, her face a study of fine wrinkles, but her eyes...her eyes as always flashing bright. She seemed to be repeating something. *The laurel. The answer's in the laurel.* Then Gran faded, replaced by the dark-robed figure on the road. The mystery lady.

Tonight, she looked very familiar, and in the dream I suddenly knew why.

The recognition jolted me awake. I sat upright in the bed, my heart pounding furiously. It was no wonder Pepper had been alarmed that first day in the Cove! Animals have a sixth sense, an almost psychic ability to recognize supernatural occurrences. Pepper had known what was strange about the mystery lady.

Forcing myself to take slow, deep breaths, I waited until my heart stopped pounding. Then I turned on the bedside lamp and picked up the old newspaper I'd left on the nightstand.

I should have known the moment I found the old photograph in the cabin. The woman in the picture, the woman on the Cove road—they were one and the same.

I sat on the edge of the bed and tried to accept this. Was it possible? Had Cissy somehow reached out to me over the chasm that separated the living from the...

Rubbing the scar just above my hairline, I swallowed hard at the sudden fear pumping through my veins. Perhaps this was all a result of the injury, some delayed reaction to having my brain jarred. I thought of calling my doctor in the morning and asking...what? If it was common to see ghosts after a concussion?

Staring down at the faded newsprint, I had to admit the truth. For some reason Cissy had chosen to reach out to me, and suddenly I felt a strange kinship with her. I made a vow then that before I left the Cove this time, I would know what really happened the night Sheridan O'Malley was laid out by the river, a cluster of laurel blossoms upon his chest.

* * *

When morning allowed me to think more clearly, I realized how difficult it might be to find more information about the sixty-five-year-old murder. Aunt Mattie had told me all she knew, and I hesitated mentioning any of this to her. As much as she was practical and pretended not to believe in ghosts, I knew she would tell me to leave the entire matter alone, which I couldn't do now that I had promised to find the truth.

There was something I had been meaning to do since I'd come back to the Cove. It seemed a good place to start my search. Gulping a cup of coffee and slice of toast, I took Pepper to the resort and set off alone in my car.

It was a glorious day, so typical of summer in the Smokies. The sun quickly burned away all traces of mist from the high-tops, and the mountains stood clear and velvet green beneath the bright blue of a flawless sky. Only a few whisps of clouds drifted over those higher peaks to cast small, lazy shadows upon the foothills, and the fragrance of a million wildflowers lay pungent in the air.

A short time later, I stopped at the churchyard where my grandparents and father were buried. I'd picked some lilacs earlier and carried them now to the gravesites that lay close together. Kneeling at each, I brushed away a few dry leaves and twigs. Gently, I laid the blossoms by the headstones and closed my eyes for a moment to ask for their help. I knew Gran and Daddy would have believed what was happening to me. They'd both held onto the old mountain folklore, had believed in the old tales.

I stood then and looked around. There were two other cemeteries in the Cove. Cissy could be buried in either of them. It didn't seem likely she would be laid to rest in this tiny churchyard, a woman reputed to be a murderess and a witch. And yet…

I walked among the other markers, noticing how they sometimes chronicled the history of the Cove. Evidence of an epidemic. A war. A time when women had seen only a few of their many children actually reach adulthood.

At the far edge of the churchyard lay a fresh grave with no marker. Could it be Cissy's? I had started back toward the parsonage to see if anyone was home when I noticed someone else walking among the graves. He turned toward me, and I realized it was Jed Hamilton.

"Morning, Jane. Paying respects to your loved ones? My wife is here, too. I like just stopping by for a visit now and then. Helps sometimes to talk things over with Sadie."

He stood with his hands in the pockets of his trousers and gazed out over the peaceful churchyard. He seemed lonely, and I wondered what sort of life he'd had. As far as I knew, he and Sadie'd had only one son who'd died while serving his country. In spite of being mayor and having the respect of the Cove residents, I didn't think he was a very happy man.

I didn't know what to say and so just asked what he knew of Cissy's final resting place.

"Why it's right over there." He pointed to the fresh grave. "The new minister here is young, and he saw no reason why she shouldn't be buried in the churchyard."

"Did…did anyone attend her service?" It pained me to think she'd been buried without anyone to grieve.

"Actually, a few did. Your aunt and uncle, a few other old-timers, and myself."

I glanced up at him, wanting to say thank you for his concern for the old woman, but the clear gray eyes were looking through me in an oddly piercing way.

"There's to be a marker delivered any day now. It wouldn't be right for her not to have one."

"I don't understand. Who's paying for it?"

He shrugged. "Why, I am. I paid for everything."

I contemplated his words a second. "How generous of you. But why? What did Cissy mean to you?"

He looked at me fully now, and a strange smile curved his mouth. "It was the least I could do. I like to take care of my people in the Cove. They depend on me, you know, and I'm obliged to look after them. Besides, Cissy had such a sad life."

I would have liked to ask him just what he did remember of Cissy's life, but he walked on past me. When I left, he was standing before the grave marked Sadie Hamilton.

I climbed back in my car and was grateful for the air

conditioning. I turned it up full blast and for a moment considered driving up into the mountains where it was certain to be cooler. Maybe now, since I knew of Cissy's final resting place, and that at least a few residents of Laurel Cove had cared enough to bid her goodbye, it would be enough. Maybe I could forget about trying to find the solution to what would long be considered a cold-case murder.

But the memory of last night's dream, and all the others before it, crowded into my mind. Before long, I left the Cove and turned onto the highway toward Pineville.

It wasn't difficult to find the office of the Gazette. I could only hope they might still have records from sixty-five years ago, papers on microfilm that might tell more than did just the single page I'd found in the cabin.

My hopes were promptly crushed. The gray-haired lady at the reception desk was as helpful as she could be, but as far as she knew nothing remained of old publications, not even a single copy dated more than fifty years ago. A fire had completely destroyed the press about that time and nothing had been salvaged. For many years there had been no local paper. The elder Mr. Kimball had started this one, to be taken over by his son about five years ago. Had she ever heard of the old woman Cissy Oliver? She confessed to having moved here only a few months ago and was only repeating what others had told her.

I thanked her for her help anyway and reluctantly pushed open the door. A blast of warm air and a solid body collided with me. Two strong hands gripped my shoulders to keep me from flying backwards.

"I'm terribly sorry," the man said, then we both

stared. From behind the black framed glasses, Deane Kimball took in my startled expression. "Jane, right? I didn't mean to just walk into you."

I assured him I was fine and tried to continue on by. He stepped back, but his gaze remained fixed on me.

"Was there something we could help you with?"

"I guess not...I was looking for information about someone, but there doesn't seem to be anything." Another person came through the door and we had to move aside. Deane took the opportunity to touch my arm and motioned with his head toward the hallway behind us.

"Come down to my office. I'll see what I can do."

Reluctantly, I followed him down the short beige-carpeted hallway. Several offices opened off of it. The editor's was the very last. It was not what one could call elegantly appointed, but the massive hand-carved mahogany desk and floor to ceiling bookshelves were impressive. I imagined they'd been here since Deane's father was editor of the *Pineville Gazette*.

Deane motioned toward a soft leather chair. While I sank into it, he perched on the corner of his desk and loosened his tie.

"So, what information did you need?" The deep brown eyes behind the glasses studied me intently. "Or are you on a mission for Brendan's group?"

"Nothing of the sort. I hoped you would have back copies of the *Gazette* on microfilm."

"Actually, we do. How far back did you want to go?"

"Sixty-five years."

Deane's eyebrows shot up an inch. "Quite a while ago. I suppose Mrs. Thomas told you about the unfortunate fire that took out the old *Gazette*. Much as I hate to say it, our history now begins when my dad started the paper up again."

"So, there is no way of researching something that happened then?"

"Are you talking about in the Cove? There are a few old-timers who would maybe talk to you. The mayor himself goes back a way. Just what is it you're researching?"

I hesitated talking about Cissy to him. Would he ridicule my interest in an old woman of Laurel Cove? He didn't seem to hold the residents of the Cove in very high regard. Certainly not those who didn't want a hotel complex in their midst. But I had to take a chance he might know something about Cissy.

"I'd like to find out more about a woman called Cissy Oliver. She lived in the Cove for many years and only died—"

"Couple months ago. Don't look surprised. I do read the obits in my paper. I heard she was a recluse of sorts. Something about being accused of a crime."

"Murder." I decided to plunge ahead. "It was thought she killed the man she was going to marry, but she was never charged. The murder remains unsolved."

"And you would like to know what really happened. Any particular reason?"

If he knew the truth of the matter, I was sure Deane Kimball would consider me totally out of it. In spite of the ghost stories that abounded throughout the mountains, he would not be a believer in them. I would have my own doubts...except I'd seen Cissy walking in the Cove and felt her presence in the cabin.

"I remember seeing Cissy when I was a child and

feeling sorry for her even then. I believe now she was unjustly accused. She lived a sad, lonely life and she died alone. That's reason enough to want to know who really killed Sheridan O'Malley."

Deane shook his head and shoved away from the desk. "I hate to say it, but you may find yourself coming up against a dead end."

Somehow, I didn't think that would happen. Why would Cissy have appeared to me if there didn't exist some way to find out the truth?

"I'll just have to keep trying. I am known for being determined once I set my mind to something."

Deane gave me a curious, almost shy smile. "Doesn't surprise me." He walked with me to the door of his office. "If I can be of help in any way, just give me a call."

He held out his hand, and I shook it. Brendan wouldn't appreciate my saying so, but Deane Kimball really didn't seem so bad after all.

As I drove back into the Cove, the weather suddenly began to change. Thick clouds shrouded the high-tops and fog soon drifted down to creep along the twisting road. Good thing I hadn't planned on this being a picture-taking excursion, because the lovely day soon vanished in the mist of rain that began to fall. I had thought this morning of bringing my camera along but hadn't been able to find it. Now I remembered why. I'd left it and the small notebook in the cabin the day I found the newspaper page. They were sitting on the little table beside the armless rocking chair. Did I dare venture there to retrieve them?

With only a moment's hesitation, I turned down the side road. When the cabin came into sight, I parked along the dirt two-track and set off on foot. Wet ferns and wildflowers slapped at my legs, and I wished now I'd worn jeans instead of white capris. I had to wonder— would I be doing this if I hadn't left the camera? I knew the answer. The lure of Cissy's cabin was simply too great, and nothing would have dissuaded me from going there again.

When I slipped inside the cabin, the damp musty odor filled my head. I glanced around, adjusting my eyes to the dimness, listening to the steady drip of rain as it leaked in. It stained the once scrubbed floor a dirty brown. A strange apprehension slithered along my spine and the urge to turn and flee took ahold of me. *Get the camera and notebook and leave.* Steadying myself, I crossed to the small armless rocker and the table beside it.

The camera and notebook were there. But why wouldn't they be? Who else would be foolhardy enough to enter this place? I picked up the camera and slung the strap over my shoulder, wishing I had the case because of the rain.

The rain. It poured now, drumming on the roof, running in rivulets across the floor. By the time I got back to my car, I'd be soaked.

Reluctantly, I sat down in the rocker and prepared to wait out the downpour. To calm myself and keep from fidgeting, I opened the notebook and flipped past the pages where I'd recorded the different wildflowers photographed the day Brendan and I went riding. Perhaps it would help to write down everything I knew about Cissy so far. I turned to the first empty page.

Only it wasn't empty. Two words slanted across the top of the page...and it was not in my hand. My breath stuck in my chest as I stared down at the fine, flourishing script and read the words. *Key wind.*

It made no sense. It also made no sense no one else had had access to this notebook but me, and yet something was written in it, and I had definitely not put it there.

A shiver rippled across my shoulders. It had nothing to do with the dank air in the cabin nor my own damp clothing. I leaned back in the armless rocker, pushing it slowly back and forth, trying to come to grips with this latest puzzle. Who had written this? It could be explained...couldn't it?

A soft plop of water landed on my shoe and drew my attention to the mantel above the barren hearth. More crystal drops formed there. Another leak had sprung, just above the small black mantel clock, a clock that had long ago wound down, never to be set again. How long had the hands been motionless? Since Cissy's death? Since Sheridan's? Had they stopped when she heard the news? Had Cissy found no use for the clock when time was no longer important? When was the last time she had put her hand to the key behind the clock to wind...the key...to wind.

Rising slowly, I put a tentative hand to the silent clock, closing my fingers around it and bringing it toward me. A thick coating of dust covered the smooth slanting sides. The folded paper fell away from between the clock and the chimney and slid quietly to the floor.

I picked it up gingerly, as if suddenly afraid of what it might contain. I held a single sheet from a ruled nickel tablet, the sort children had once used in school. Folded once, it lay in my hand yellowed and crumbling as the newspaper I'd taken from the drawer. Would it fall to pieces if I opened it? No, Cissy had intended for me to find it. It was the reason for the words written in my notebook. Maybe the reason for my being drawn to the cabin in the first place.

The overpowering scent of flowers suddenly filled the room. I sat down in the rocker and carefully unfolded the paper.

The message was written in a firm bold hand and showed clear on the page even after all this time.

Dear Cissy,

I feel so bad for what has happened to you. It's so unfair. You didn't kill Sheridan. I know it, because I saw who shot Sheridan. I don't know his name, but he comes from the other side of the ridge. He looks like one of the weasels Samuel catches in the chicken coop. His eyes are small and cold. They remind me of the fog off the mountains. I was out picking flowers. I heard him talking to Sheridan that night by the river. He sounded mad. I got scared and hid behind some laurel bushes, but I kept peeking out. Their voices got louder. Sheridan started to walk away. Old weasel-face called out and Sheridan turned around. That's when it happened. I saw the gun and I almost called out, but it was too late. He shot Sheridan just once. Then he walked over and looked at him where he lay on the ground. He laughed and stuck the gun in his pocket and walked away. When he was gone, I crept out and looked too. Sheridan looked just like he was sleeping, but I knew he was dead. There was a little hole right over his heart and the blood had already stained his shirt. I started to cry and what I did wasn't right. It's why they think you did it. I put the cluster of laurel blossoms I'd picked on his chest, to cover the hole. I don't know why I did it. Maybe because

I didn't want you to see him that way, if you found him. I want to tell the truth, Cissy. You've been a good friend to me. Please tell me what to do.

Signed,

Thea.

I closed my eyes and sighed. Gran's name was Althea. Could this letter have been from my own grandmother? Had she known all along who really killed Sheridan? To think she hadn't told the truth and thus saved Cissy a lifetime of loneliness tugged at my heart. In keeping silent, a murderer had gone free.

About the time the rain ceased drumming on the cabin roof, the scent of flowers drifted away. Clutching the notebook, camera, and now the precious letter, I made my way quickly back to the car.

Chapter 8

The fog lifted in the evening, and Brendan stopped by to ask if I wanted to see a movie in Pineville. I'd been sitting at the kitchen table, reading over the last three pages of manuscript I'd written, when he knocked at the back door.

"I guess I keep interrupting your work." He straddled one of the wooden chairs and gave me a sheepish grin. "But you know what they say about all work and no play."

Seeing the teasing light in his turquoise eyes, I said coyly, "No, what do they say?"

"I don't know. I never asked them. But it must be something like best make hay while the sun shines."

I groaned at his clichés.

"I really need to work, Brendan. I already asked for an extension on my deadline."

"I thought you were supposed to be down here for a few weeks of R and R. Of course, Mattie did say you were out traipsing about all afternoon. Where'd you wander off to?"

Should I tell him about the letter and the strange things I'd experienced since coming back to the Cove? Could I trust him to believe I wasn't crazy? I wasn't sure yet.

"I just drove around, stopped in at the cemetery to visit Gran and my dad. Then the weather turned nasty."

"Well, it's a beautiful night now. If you're not up to a movie, we could go for ice cream. My treat."

It was like we were back in high school, except I didn't remember Brendan ever being quite so accommodating then. "Well, if it's chocolate almond you're talking about."

He winked and, in a moment, had pulled me from my chair.

"Whatever your heart desires. You can even bring that fuzzball you call a dog along for the ride."

Pepper enjoyed herself immensely, sitting behind my seat, letting the cool night air blow the long hair back from her face. On the way to the ice cream shop in town, Brendan told me about the Laurel Cove League's plans to protest in Pineville the following week. Apparently, Stefanie's group had been hard at work. I expected him to be enthused about the whole venture, but I sensed it was not the way he wanted to fight the issue. He abruptly changed the subject and began to tell me about the group of high school students he would be taking into the mountains soon.

"They're a great group of kids and a real joy to work with. I'm looking forward to the trip as much as they are."

This was the type of teaching he truly enjoyed, and I could just imagine this big, rough man instructing young people in the ways of the mountains he so loved.

In spite of my interest in what he had to say, I couldn't help but keep glancing at the side of the road, wondering if I would see Cissy walking tonight. I'd almost come to expect it. She would know I'd been back to the cabin and read the letter from Gran. But what did she want me to do about it?

"I guess you were serious about being involved in your work. Or am I boring you to death?"

I pulled my attention from outside and turned to look at the man driving. I longed to tell him about everything. Maybe I just had to take a chance.

"It's not that," I said softly. "Something's been happening to me, ever since I came back to the Cove. I'm sure you'll think I've a screw or two loose."

His brows pulled together in a frown. "If it's got to do with what happened in New York—"

"It doesn't. It's about something that happened here…sixty-five years ago."

He shook his head. "I don't follow."

I tried to think where to begin, but then in a sudden torrent it all poured out. In a few moments I'd told him about everything—the woman on the road, the strange lure of the cabin, the dreams, and finally the letter in which my grandmother had admitted to knowing who really committed the murder.

"It's true, Brendan. Gran saw who killed Sheridan. It wasn't Cissy."

"Shouldn't it be enough then? You've got the truth you wanted."

"Not all of it." I searched for the right words to make him understand. "Why didn't Gran tell someone? Why did she let Cissy carry the blame? My grandmother was a strong woman. She would have stood up for what was right. Something kept her quiet."

"What does it matter now? What difference will it make? Everyone who was involved with what happened then is probably gone. So why should it matter?"

"It matters to me. Gran wanted to tell the truth, but she didn't. Cissy could have pleaded innocent, but she didn't. Why? I would just like to know." I didn't add this must be the key to helping Cissy find her rest.

"I suppose next you'll be trying to find out who the man was that shot Sheridan."

"If only I could."

"Did you ever stop and think maybe he had it coming to him? I'd always understood Sheridan was a rogue, a lady's man. Chances are, he courted danger and maybe was involved in illegal dealings—gambling, running bootleg whiskey. It was probably only a matter of time before he got it. Could be he was even shot by one of his own people if they suspected him of working with the feds. You know how mountain folk feel about traitors."

I didn't think this was so about Sheridan, that he'd been a traitor, but I only said, "Maybe you're right. I just think there must be some other clue."

Brendan shook his head but said no more.

At the ice cream shop, I ordered a double scoop of chocolate almond in a waffle cone for me and a baby vanilla cone for Pepper. We sat at an outside table, watching the summer visitors come and go. When a group of young people sauntered by, I recognized Jeff and Stefanie. I hoped she wouldn't notice us, but of course those sharp green eyes missed nothing. I groaned inwardly when she left the group and bounced over.

"Oh hi. Out for a drive? We just saw a movie, but it was pretty dull. 'Course maybe you would like it." She looked pointedly at me. I took it to mean I was pretty dull. "Do you suppose they have low fat ice cream here? I really shouldn't even have it. You're lucky you can eat the chocolate stuff. I'd be a mess if I did."

I glanced from Stefanie, in her skinny designer jeans

that left several inches of bare skin between them and her skimpy knit top, to the remnants of my cone. She sure knew how to get her digs in.

"Oh, by the way, I saw you earlier in town today, coming out of the newspaper office. It looked like Deane Kimball was with you, but maybe I'm wrong. I waved, but I guess you didn't see me."

Brendan eyed me while Stefanie just smiled sweetly and went back to join her friends. An uneasy silence fell while we finished our cones.

I glanced at him. A frown creased his brow.

"Go ahead and ask it," I murmured.

"Ask what?"

"Why was I at the *Gazette* and why was I talking to Deane Kimball."

He sat silent a moment, then said, "It's none of my business."

Which might be true but I would tell him anyway. "I was hoping to find some information about Cissy in any old newspapers they might have, but no luck. All old records and papers were lost years ago in a fire. Maybe I have the only one left from that time."

"And Deane helped you personally."

I shrugged. "He really couldn't, but he seemed interested in the story of Cissy. If I could just piece together what happened sixty-five years ago, maybe Deane would run a story in the *Gazette*. At least then everybody would know Cissy really wasn't a witch or a murderer."

He mulled this over and after a little while we headed back to the four-wheel drive. I saw Jeff's van pulling onto the highway just before I noticed the slip of paper stuck beneath the windshield wiper. Brendan reached out and pulled it free.

"What is it?" I peered past his arm and read the three words before he crumpled the paper. *Give it up.*

"Why that little—"

Brendan's head jerked up, and he pinned me with his piercing gaze. "You know who left this?"

"Isn't it obvious? I just can't believe Stefanie would stoop to this kind of prank."

"You think Stefanie did it?" He smoothed the paper and considered the hastily scribbled note again. He shook his head. "Why would she? You saw how enthusiastic she is about working with the League. She's even going to lead the protest."

He thought the note was directed at him, planted by someone who wanted him to give up his fight against Harrison Enterprises. After lifting Pepper into the vehicle, I took the wrinkled note from him.

"I don't think this has anything to do with the League. It's the trick of a girl who's seeing the old green-eyed monster. Stefanie has been three shades of the color ever since she saw me with you. This is her way of telling me, hands off."

"That's ridiculous."

"Is it? Do you deny she's attracted to you?"

"Well, maybe she is, a little, but…"

"Not a little, Brendan, a lot." I fought a sudden dryness in my throat. "The girl is smitten with you. You're a hero to her. But I don't appreciate her threatening me."

"I'd hardly call this a threat." He turned the key and backed out of the parking space. "And I don't believe it's Stefanie's work, no matter what you say."

"Then whose work would you say it is?"

"Someone who's determined I quit fighting these developers. Someone who wants them here for his own selfish gain. Kimball knows what I drive."

"I think we would have noticed him pull up. Besides, Deane doesn't seem the type to leave nasty notes on people's windshields."

He gave me a curious sideways glance. "So, you already know what type he is?"

I didn't want to pursue the conversation further and so just kept silent. When Brendan brought me home, he only brushed a quick kiss across my forehead for a goodnight. Feeling he had tossed my own concerns aside, I tucked Pepper under my arm and hurried inside the house.

Before going to bed, I sat in the silence of my room and studied the old letter and the newspaper with its faded photo of Cissy Oliver. Tonight, something else about the picture bothered me, a resemblance I couldn't quite place. I could see the dark-robed lady and the sad face, but her eyes, though blurred with time, reminded me of another's.

* * *

Aunt Mattie came by the next day with a cardboard carton held in her arms.

"I was poking around in a closet yesterday and found these. Thought maybe you should be the one to have them."

I peered into the box she set on the table and saw a stack of spiral notebooks, obviously very written in. Plucking one out, I blew dust from its cover and read the name written on it.

Jack Stuart.

"Daddy's? These were all his?"

My aunt nodded. "He always fancied putting his thoughts down on paper from the time he was a boy. You being a writer and all, I thought you'd like to see them."

I ran my hand thoughtfully over the notebook cover. "I never knew. I don't recall ever seeing him writing."

"He liked to go off by himself. I guess it helped him relax. He never let any of us read what he put down, not even your mama. She found these notebooks after he died, when she had to go through his things. She couldn't bring herself to read them, but she asked me not to throw them away. I've thought about them over the years, but I never was sure if I had the right to read them either. If Jack had wanted us to know, he would've shown us when he was alive."

"Why have you brought them out now?" I clutched the notebook to me, as if by doing so I could hold my father close again.

Aunt Mattie shrugged. "The time just seems right, and if anybody ever reads them, it should be you." She smiled wistfully, and I thought I saw a tear glisten in her eye. I knew Mattie had dearly loved my father, her twin brother, and even after fifteen years she missed him very much. "Seems a shame if no one ever knows what he wrote about."

She turned to leave, but I caught her back and gave her a hug. "Thank you," I whispered, unable to trust my own voice.

Later, I sat in the cool shaded living room and opened the first notebook. To my surprise, I discovered a number of stories that had been handed down among families of the Cove. Some were stories about the folk who had first settled these mountains. Others told of the beauty and mystery of the Smokies. A number of superstitions were included, a few downright ghost stories. I recognized them as the stories Daddy had often told us girls.

As I went from one notebook to the next, I began to see how my father had actually planned this to be a book about Laurel Cove and its legends. It must have taken him a long time, maybe even years, to chronicle these stories, and it was sad the project had remained unfinished, cut short by his untimely death.

It made me ache inside, and then I wondered—had he known about Cissy and Sheridan? Had Gran told him the story, and had Jack Stuart lived, would he have included it in his book?

In the very last notebook, I finally found mention of them. Only a few short paragraphs and they told me nothing more than I already knew. And yet I had the feeling my father had wished he knew more about these two people, as if their story was somehow more personal to him. The strangest thing of all was the last line written in the notebook.

I know exactly how Cissy must feel. I have always felt like an outsider, like I've never truly been part of this family or the Cove.

What an odd thing. My father had grown up here, been raised in this very house. Why should he have felt out of place in Laurel Cove?

Feeling more confused than ever, I piled the notebooks back in the carton and carried them up to my room.

I didn't see Brendan that day, and I couldn't help but wonder if he was with Stefanie, planning their protest. I was too old for silly jealousies, but the picture of them working together wouldn't leave my mind.

My own work was the best distraction from disturbing thoughts. Propping myself on the sofa, Pepper at my feet, I balanced the laptop on my knees and delved into the manuscript. Several hours later, I finished chapter six. The story was starting to come together but lacked the compelling factor that had won my last book the award. Niggling doubts picked at my brain. Perhaps I'd somehow lost my writing ability after all. Lydia expected a call from me this week, just to let her know how I was doing. Since my cell phone didn't work well here, and I needed to make a trip to the grocery in Pineville, I decided tomorrow would be soon enough to call New York.

When I lay in bed, with the crickets chirping in rhythm and a tree frog singing right outside my window, New York with its honking taxis and screaming sirens seemed very far away. Little by little, I was beginning to slip back into the Cove way of life and the truth was, I really didn't mind this slower pace. Nothing else seemed very important now—not my career, not even the people who knew and cared about me in the city. I just wanted to be in this room, in this big four poster bed, with the summer breeze fluttering the curtains and the fragrance of mountain laurel drifting in the night.

My last thought before falling asleep was, how strange that my father, born in the Cove, had not believed himself a part of it at all.

Chapter 9

The next day, I decided to talk to Aunt Mattie about the strange things I'd been experiencing. I found her on the bungalow's front porch and drew up a chair while she worked on the quilt she planned to enter in the craft show.

For a while, I just watched her nimble fingers at work. Then I asked the question that had been uppermost in my mind since I first found the article about Cissy in the cabin.

"Aunt Mattie, is there any special reason why Cecilia is my first name?"

She never missed a stitch, but I saw a tiny frown crease her brow. "If I remember right, it was your Gran's idea. She seemed to favor the name, though none of us knew quite why."

"And Mother didn't protest?"

"She did at first. She had Jane picked out for months, because her favorite book was *Jane Eyre*, but your daddy sweet-talked her into adding the Cecilia. It's a pretty name, I always thought."

If I told Mattie my name and Cissy's were the same, and Gran and the old recluse had been linked in a tragic way, she would wonder how I knew. If I told her I'd been in the cabin again, she might be upset. But how else was I to understand this whole bizarre situation?

"Cissy Oliver's name was Cecilia," I said matter-offactly. "Did you know that?"

Now her fingers stilled and she looked up at me. "I...I don't recall anyone ever calling her anything but Cissy."

"Witch Cissy," I murmured, then took a deep breath and continued. "I have to tell you something, something I've discovered about Cissy Oliver...and Gran." I went on to explain about the picture of Cissy and the letter. At the last minute, I decided not to mention I was certain I'd seen the spirit of Cissy Oliver walking in the Cove. I was having trouble coping with that notion.

"Do you think someone would have frightened Gran into not talking? She always seemed such a strong woman to me."

"And she was!" Aunt Mattie declared. "But I think it came from having to raise two little ones alone. You know your grandfather died when Jack and I were just tots. A farm accident left him with a terrible injury that finally took him. Your Gran started this resort by herself. What came before we were born, I couldn't tell you."

I knew she didn't enjoy talking about this, and I didn't want to upset her. She and Uncle Theo had been acting a bit strange the past few days, as if they were worried about something. Perhaps if the hotel complex was built in the Cove, it would be the end of the resort?

A late model sedan pulled into the drive. Jed Hamilton unfolded his tall spare frame from behind the wheel and strode toward the porch. He stopped at the steps and tipped his cap to us.

"Good mornin', ladies." He nodded courteously toward us. "Just thought I'd let you know that I took up the matter of the phone calls with the police chief in Pineville. He said if it happens again, you're to let him know immediately. He could have a tracer put on your phone."

I glanced quizzically at my aunt. Her fingers fumbled and she jabbed the needle into her hand.

"What calls?" I demanded, looking from Mattie to the mayor. "What is he talking about?"

The mayor's eyebrows peaked in surprise. "I thought you'd told your niece about the threats. Didn't you think she should know?"

Aunt Mattie pulled a flowered hanky from her pocket and dabbed at the pinpoint of blood on her finger. "I didn't think she needed to know. Jane's been through enough trauma. She came down here to rest, not to get involved with our problems."

I scooted my chair closer and touched her arm. "Aunt Mattie, your problems are my problems, too. Whatever affects Laurel Cove, affects me. When I first learned Gran left me her house, I didn't have an idea what I'd do with it. But I think now I'd like to keep it, have a place to escape to from time to time. So, I am concerned with whatever happens here, and most of all, if you've been threatened in any way."

"You should tell her, Mattie." Jed came up onto the porch and lay a reassuring hand on my aunt's shoulder. "And then I don't want either of you to worry about this. I'm going to speak to Chief Miller again and ask that he have an officer patrol the Cove more frequently, just in case there's anyone suspicious hanging around. You know I always take care of my people."

As soon as he'd left, I insisted Aunt Mattie tell me what sort of threats they'd received.

"Oh, at first they were just nuisance calls. You know the sort, the phone rings and no one's there. Then some gravelly-voiced character starts saying, 'You can't stop them. It's too late. Give it up.'"

"'Them meaning?"

"Harrison Enterprises for sure. We're not the only folks in the Cove to get the calls, but it seems we get them more often. Maybe because our land adjoins the river. It's a prime location."

"Do you think someone's trying to scare you into selling?"

Aunt Mattie shrugged. "I don't know, but they're going have to try harder than that. Theo and I aren't about to sell out." She stopped a moment and pursed her usually smiling mouth tight, I thought to keep back the tears. Her voice trembled. "This…this place is our life and no one's going to force us out."

I leaned over and hugged her sturdy frame. "Me either," I murmured.

While walking back to the farmhouse, it dawned on me. The note on Brendan's windshield the night before had said the same thing, *give it up.* So maybe he was right and the note was directed at him. Who in the Cove was not above threatening notes and phone calls? Could it be someone from Harrison Enterprises? A shady way to do business, but depending how bad they wanted to build their hotel here, anything was possible.

Later, I drove into Pineville and made my call to New York.

Yes, Lydia, I said, *I'm feeling better. Yes, I'm working. No, I don't think I'll be returning sooner than planned. I can send you the chapters I have so far but I really need to take the whole month here.* Had I mentioned any of the strange things going on in the Cove, she would have certainly thought I was getting worse instead of better.

I stopped at the Pineville Drugstore to pick up shampoo and toothpaste and then the hardware for a pair of clippers to trim the lilac bushes. I asked the clerk where I might find a copy machine. I'd decided to make copies of both the old letter and the newspaper in case something should happen to the originals. At the moment both were safely tucked into a folder in my oversized shoulder bag, but I knew the less I handled them the better.

The clerk pointed me to a slightly archaic machine in the back of the store and assured me it worked fine. While feeding the cranky machine quarters, I overheard someone talking on the phone in the store's office. I couldn't be quite certain, but it sounded like Jed. Something about his voice caught my attention. He spoke low but in a firm tone, as if he sought to convince the listener. Curious, I strained to hear what he said.

"Yes…yes, I know, but I tell you, my way is the best. I know how to deal with them, and there's no reason…"

The clerk came to the back of the store with another customer, looking for a garden hose, and I lost the rest of the conversation. I took some time shuffling the copies I'd made into a folder, stalling for time. If it was Jed on the phone, I wanted to speak with him about the calls Mattie and Theo had received. A few minutes later I heard a door in the back open and click closed.

When she finished with the customer, the clerk, a dark-haired woman perhaps in her late thirties, came over to see if I was having trouble.

"No, everything's fine," I glanced at her nametag, "Ella." I closed the folder, reluctant to have her see the copies. I looked around the store, noting how some of the merchandise looked like it had been there since I was a kid. Hamilton's Hardware had a little bit of everything, but I wondered just how Jed managed to stay afloat. "How is business these days?"

I saw her dart a quick look toward the office before she realized we were alone in the store. She whispered, "Not so good this past year, I'm afraid. Folks would rather go to the big discount shopping center ten miles up the highway."

"Seems a shame. Jed's put his whole life into this place." Just like Theo and Mattie with the resort.

She shrugged. "I wouldn't be surprised to see him close the store before long. He's hardly ever in here, and when he is..." She stopped, as if afraid someone would overhear. She sighed before going back to her work. I suspected that, despite the goodwill he seemed to profess, Jedidiah wasn't the easiest man to have for a boss.

The summer day had grown increasingly hot and humid, and it didn't surprise me to hear thunder rumbling over the mountains. By the time I reached the highway, the sky had darkened to an ominous hue. I debated briefly whether to try and make it back to the Cove before the storm hit and quickly decided I'd rather not drive the twisting roads in a downpour. Luckily, Shirley's Diner was straight ahead. I pulled into the parking area and left my car, sprinting inside just as the first giant drops hit the pavement.

Inside, the comforting smell of fresh coffee and pies baking led me to the lunch counter. Seating myself, I plucked a plastic covered menu from between the salt and pepper shakers. Was I hungry enough to eat a sandwich? I'd almost decided when someone spoke.

"The cheese and potato soup is really very good, but if it's just dessert you want, I'd always recommend the coconut cream pie."

I glanced up. Deane Kimball sat at the end of the counter, plunging a fork into an ample slice of pie. Minus a suit jacket, with his shirtsleeves rolled up and tie slightly askew, he reminded me of an eager high school boy.

"It looks good," I admitted and asked the waitress to bring me a slice and some coffee. Deane finished off his pie and a large glass of milk before speaking again.

"So, what brings you into town, still looking for information about the old woman?" He leaned both arms on the counter and studied me curiously from behind his thick framed glasses.

"I'm thinking now if there is anything to be found about Cissy, it won't be in Pineville. I doubt she left the Cove after the...after what happened." I sipped my coffee and hoped he would drop the subject. It was too much to ask of a newspaper man.

"Could be that rundown cabin where she lived holds some secrets about the old gal. 'Course, who would want to snoop around in there? I've heard the place is haunted."

What would he think if he knew I'd been there, had experienced a presence other than my own and had indeed found old secrets...secrets leading only to more questions.

"Now, I wonder what would happen to a certain developer's plans if it got around Laurel Cove is haunted? Would it be a plus or a minus?"

I set down my fork and met Deane's frank gaze.

"What do you mean?"

"Well, you know there is a segment of the population who would be in the Cove in an instant if they thought something paranormal was happening. Ghost hunters are always looking for the next haunted spot. On the other hand, I doubt you'd bring in many All-American type families. I'm not sure to which group Harrison would rather appeal. I suppose, whoever would spend the most money."

I pushed the unfinished pie away and asked the waitress for my check. Suddenly it turned my stomach to think of the dubious future Laurel Cove might suffer if indeed Harrison Enterprises had its way.

"I sincerely hope," I said, counting out the correct money from my wallet, "it never gets to that point."

In spite of the rain, I left the diner and hurried back to my car. The storms continued the remainder of the day and into the evening. Just after sundown, they dissipated, the thunder fading away over the mountains. Pepper and I sat on the porch and watched the last jags of lightening flicker in the sky to the west. The night was sultry, and the scents of lilac and rain and the river mingled in the air. I pushed the old swing back and forth, listening to it creak softly in time to the insects that buzzed and whirred.

I usually didn't mind being alone, but tonight I found myself wishing it wasn't just Pepper who sat with me. What was Brendan doing tonight? Did it bother him at all that we'd parted uneasily? Did how I felt about anything matter to him?

If only he'd stopped by. If only I didn't feel so alone.

And then, at Pepper's soft growl and a rustling in the nearby bushes, I knew I wasn't alone.

Chapter 10

At the end of the porch, the lilac bushes rustled softly. Something stirred from them. My skin prickled, and I hoped it was only those infamous bunnies playing games. But a shadow separated itself from the cover of the bush and it was no bunny. It moved stealthily toward the morning glory-covered trellis, then to the steps. I held my breath and gently placed my hand on Pepper's head where she lay on the swing beside me.

A low growl rumbled from her throat.

"Shhshh," I whispered and watched the shadow climb the steps, cross the porch, and reach for the screen door. He didn't see us in the darkened corner of the porch, and I wondered fleetingly if I should just keep silent and escape while he was inside. I shuddered at the thought of him wandering in my house, and heaven knew what he wanted anyway. The matter was settled when Pepper growled again and shifted closer to me. The swing creaked.

He swung about on unsteady feet, his squinty eyes searching for us in the dark. No doubt he'd been drinking again, and I figured the best way to handle this situation was to get the upper hand.

"Why are you here, Gil?" I asked, rising from the swing while Pepper continued to growl.

"Miz Al—hic—thea?" He staggered toward me.

I steeled myself against feeling sorry for him.

Sympathy would do little good here.

"You know Gran's gone, Gil. She's not here anymore."

He was close enough for me to smell the liquor on his breath. My stomach roiled. He'd probably been drinking for most of the evening, enough to make him forget my grandmother, who'd once been kind to him, was gone.

He sagged against the porch railing. "I forgot. I jus' needed...to see her again." He put one hand to his head, as if trying to think clearly. "She always listened...to me."

"I miss her too." I tried to offer some small comfort to the man. "But you must realize she's in heaven now. She's happy."

He nodded and started to turn away, then, as if remembering something, he paused. "He...he told me to do something, but I can't remember now. He'll be mad, call me stupid." He looked at me pleadingly. "I'm not stupid."

"Of course, you're not." But who had called Gil stupid? Surely not Uncle Theo.

I fought against the panic when he moved closer.

"If I go back, he'll yell. Could I stay here? I won't be no bother."

The fear I thought I'd conquered suddenly gripped me again, and I had to force words past the knot in my throat. "I don't think that's a good idea. Maybe Uncle Theo would let you stay over there." I hated to foist him off on them, but I was sure they'd dealt with him like this before.

"You're nice, Miz Jane. Jus' like your gramma. Bet you wouldn't yell at me." He lurched toward me then, and my heart thudded wildly.

Pepper barked, startling Gil. He started to fall, and I took the moment to snatch up the little dog and sprint past him. If I could get my car keys in the house, I'd go to the resort for help.

I'd just reached the screen door when headlights illuminated the driveway. By the time I realized it was Brendan's vehicle, I'd re-lived the paralyzing nightmare in my apartment.

He came up onto the porch and sensed immediately something was wrong. "Jane, what is it?" His warm hands cupped my shoulders, then he realized I was staring and his eyes followed my line of vision.

Gil sat sprawled against the side of the house, his chin dropping forward onto his chest. I sagged, but strong hands held me up and steered me into the house.

"Sit here while I take care of him," he commanded and pushed me down on the sofa. Pepper squirmed and I let her go. She didn't bark at Brendan but followed as he went back out to the porch. I heard some shuffling sounds and Brendan's firm low voice. The vehicle started again, drove away, and then it was quiet. So quiet.

Wrapping my arms around myself, I leaned back on the sofa and breathed slow and deep, forcing myself to be calm, trying to recall the relaxing techniques the counselor in New York had taught me.

By the time he returned, Aunt Mattie in tow, I could breathe normally again.

"Oh my dear girl." Mattie sat beside me and took one of my hands between both her own, patting it gently. "I'm so sorry this happened. I don't know what got into Gil to come over here so late at night."

"He's looking for Gran, and it's not your fault. I

know he wouldn't have hurt me, but it's just—"

"After what you went through," she sympathized. "Of course, I understand. Are you sure you're all right, dear?"

"I'm fine. Truly." I glanced up to where Brendan stood behind us, his brows knitted together in a frown. "What…did you do with…Gil?"

"Theo's letting him sleep it off in one of the cabins. I would have taken him home, but he didn't want to go, begged me not to take him."

"He said someone yelled at him and called him stupid. Who do you suppose would do that?"

"I can't imagine," Aunt Mattie insisted. "Folks in the Cove have always been tolerant of Gil." She shrugged her shoulders and patted my hand once more. "How about I make us some nice hot tea? Brendan, you come over here and sit with Jane while I'm in the kitchen."

When my aunt had gone, he eased himself down beside me on the sofa. His presence had certainly helped calm my distress, but I wondered why he had shown up here in the first place.

I laced my fingers together and studied them a moment before asking, "How did you happen to come by tonight?"

I heard him sigh, but I didn't look at him.

"I needed to see you. I wanted to say I'm sorry for not being more concerned about your…about what you've been going through. I've gotten so wrapped up with this League business, it's sometimes all I think about. But whatever has been going on with you, and this woman you've seen, I just want you to know I care."

I dared to meet his gaze then. His turquoise eyes burned brightly, and I sank into their depths. "Thank you," I murmured and caught my breath when he leaned closer. My eyes fluttered shut and when his lips touched mine, I floated into a world where nothing mattered but the strength and caring of this man.

When the kiss ended, it seemed right to nestle into the curve of his arm, my head resting on his shoulder. By the time the tea kettle whistled in the kitchen, the night's terror had eased.

A short time later, Brendan hesitated at the door before leaving to see Aunt Mattie home.

"Are you sure you'll be okay here?" He drew me to him, and I hooked my arms around his neck. "Maybe you ought to just move in at the resort. I'm sure you'd feel more at ease. I know I would."

I rested my forehead against his bearded chin. "Perhaps, but if every time I get spooked by something I run, I'll never get past the fear. I can't let it rule my life."

His mouth moved over the scar just above my hairline and a warm shiver rushed through me. "If you're sure, but I want you to lock the doors. I know this is Laurel Cove, but too much is going on that I don't like, and I don't mean just Gil's unwelcome visits."

I wondered if he knew about the threatening calls my aunt and uncle had received. Or had other things been going on, too?

"The back door is already locked. I'll take care of this one as soon as you leave," I promised.

"Mmmmm, which I suppose I should do. I don't want Mattie to set off by herself. And she would, just to leave us alone together."

My aunt as matchmaker; yes, the title fit her quite nicely.

He seemed reluctant to let me go, and when he

kissed me this time, it was a long and slow business. When he finally lifted his lips from mine, I hesitated even opening my eyes. Then I did and saw the blue fire in his. For a moment, we were both silent.

"I almost forgot." He stepped away. "I'm taking a trip over to North Carolina tomorrow, and I thought maybe you'd like to come along. We could make a day of it, visit the museum in Cherokee, drive through the mountains."

"Sounds wonderful, but what's in North Carolina?"

"Group of folks who want to start something like our League. They've got developers threatening to put in condos and a shopping mall. I told them I'd meet with them and give whatever advice I could."

Perhaps getting away from the Cove for a few hours was a good idea. I agreed to be ready by nine.

* * *

When morning peeked over the mountains, I managed to put what had happened the night before out of my mind. Brendan showed up right on time, looking very handsome in less-faded brown cords and a plaid, open-neck shirt. The sunlight fairly glinted off his fiery hair. In the kitchen, he took my hand and drew me close to him.

"Did you sleep okay?" With one finger, he traced my jawline and then bent to give me a quick kiss.

A little breathless, I leaned against him. "Okay. Do you suppose Gil will come back here?"

"Theo promised to keep him extra busy on some new painting projects. He mentioned talking with Jedidiah about Gil, to see what kind of help they can get him. The drinking is getting out of hand."

I agreed and went for my shoulder bag and camera.

I wondered briefly if my jeans, T-shirt, and sneakers were appropriate attire, but the way Brendan was apt to stop along the road for a spontaneous hike, dressier clothes certainly wouldn't do.

We planned to leave Pepper at the resort again, so I roused her from her morning nap and snapped on her leash. When I met Brendan outside, he was brushing his hands together and frowning.

I asked, "What's wrong?"

"Flat tire. I must have picked up a nail somewhere. Just hang tight while I change it."

"If you don't mind, we could take my car. I just filled the gas tank the other day, and it's really very economical. It'll save time changing your tire right now."

He rubbed his beard thoughtfully, then shrugged. "I suppose I could fold myself into that contraption if I try, but I'll let you do the driving."

Chapter 11

In North Carolina, we met with the folks of Deer Creek. They too were determined to keep their corner of the mountains as natural as possible. I couldn't blame them. A delightfully rustic community of about five hundred, Deer Creek included a number of craftsmen and women and before we left, Brendan and I visited several, one a wood-carver who made original toys from pine blocks, another who specialized in cherry wood rockers. I bought several of the wooden toys and puzzles for Maureen's kids.

We stopped for lunch in Cherokee and Brendan asked me to drop him off in town to take care of some other business, while I spent the rest of the afternoon at the Native American museum. I browsed the selection of books for sale, many on ghostly legends of the mountains. I bought several, wishing I could have seen a book by my father among them.

Blue mists of early evening stole down from the high-tops when we started for home. We stopped near a small waterfall where a thicket of laurel grew, profusely pink. I wandered close to catch its delicate perfume, and it instantly reminded me of the mystery I'd not solved. The incident with Gil and my growing feelings for Brendan had overshadowed my concern for Cissy, but standing near the laurel, her favorite flower, I renewed my promise to her, to the elusive presence I'd felt in the cabin in the woods.

The road climbed into the bristly pine country, and the mountains quickly became shrouded in unearthly clouds, but there was no problem yet with visibility.

When he asked about the books I'd bought, I decided to tell him about the notebooks Aunt Mattie had given to me.

"My father must have collected stories for years, planning to put them into a book. I only wish he'd been able to finish it. He even mentioned Cissy and Sheridan. He said he understood why she felt out of place in the Cove. Do you think he knew something more about them?"

"Could be. Maybe you ought to think about putting the stories into a book yourself."

Coming from Brendan, the idea surprised—and tantalized—me.

"If only I could do that. And if I could find out the truth about Cissy and Sheridan, I would write their story and then everyone would know the truth."

I was so enthused about the whole idea, it took a second to register. Something was very wrong. Descending into one of the many small valleys nestled between the slopes, I applied the brakes. At first they were spongy, and then my foot went down to the floor. A sickening sensation hit my stomach.

I gripped the wheel fiercely. "The brakes... Brendan, they're gone! We can't stop!"

The car quickly picked up speed on the downhill course, an especially steep grade with only the mountain on one side and a sheer drop into air on the other.

Later, I could be thankful for his cool-headed thinking and knowledge of these mountain roads. He reached over a calm and steady hand and placed it next to mine on the steering wheel.

"Keep your nerve, Ceely Jane. We'll steer it out. There's a truck ramp just a bit farther on. We'll take it."

"Truck ramp?" My voice came out a hoarse whisper.

"Hill of soft dirt for stopping runaway trucks. It will serve us too, if we don't panic."

Panic...panic. Mustn't panic. Keep your head...hold the wheel...look straight ahead...not at the drop-off.

The mist grew thicker, the road more treacherous every foot we covered, and an eternity of minutes whizzed by before a green sign loomed ahead.

"There. There it is, another five-hundred feet." Straining against his seat belt, he moved closer to me, reaching for the steering wheel with both hands. "Just...okay...okay...get ready...now!"

As if he didn't trust me to obey, he jerked the car to the right and it left the pavement. I heard gravel spewing behind us and then with a bone-jarring thud the front tires buried themselves in the earthen barrier just as the airbags went off with a deafening bang.

Then all was quiet, save for the continued spinning of a tire in the dirt. Thrown back against the seat, I smelled rubber burning and felt Brendan's hand searching for mine when the airbags deflated.

"Are you...are you all right?"

I pinched myself to make sure. "I think so. Are you?"

It seemed a miracle neither of us was hurt, other than being badly shaken.

Finally, he said, "We should get out. Let's try your door."

It balked at first but finally gave way, screeching as

he forced it.

"Do you suppose it's totaled? It's Maureen's. She let me borrow it." I stared at my sister's car, now bent into a weird contortion.

He walked around and surveyed the damage. "Hope the insurance premiums are paid. It doesn't look good."

It hardly seemed to matter. What mattered more was that we'd survived. But now we were stranded in the mountains, with night coming on and mist curling in damp eddies around my ankles. I looked up at the tall pines looming eerily, the mountain towering above us. Turning, I stumbled to the side of the road and sank down, hugging my knees. In a delayed reaction, I found myself shaking.

Brendan dropped down beside me, wrapped his arms around me and drew me to him.

"Take it easy. It's all right." His voice was low and soothing. "We're okay."

"But…we could have…the car might have…"

"But it didn't, and what we've got to do now is figure out where we go from here."

I took a deep breath, let it out slowly, then asked, "What *are* we going to do?"

He had pulled out his phone and was checking the zero bars of service. "Well, we could walk on for a ways, look for some sort of shelter, but it's a long walk down this mountain. Or we could wait here and hope someone comes along."

Neither choice held much appeal. With the mist growing thicker by the minute, I doubted many drivers would come along through the mountains tonight. Yet the thought of walking out of here sent my pulse racing. Bears inhabited the Smokies, and I didn't relish running into one. I leaned against Brendan and sighed.

"You're the mountain expert. What would you recommend?"

Before he had a chance to reply, we heard the sound of tires on the damp roadway. They drew near, slowed, and stopped at the edge of the pavement. Through the mist I could just barely make out the shape of a light-colored sedan.

"I'll be darned," he whispered close to my ear. "It's Jedidiah."

In the glare of the sedan's headlights, Jedidiah Hamilton got out and walked toward my car. Brendan stood quickly, bringing me along with him.

"Yo, over here."

Jed peered through the mist. "Who's there? This your car?"

"It's mine," I managed to speak up as we walked toward him. Brendan kept hold of my hand.

"Brendan, is that you? What on earth happened here?"

When we stood before the mayor of Laurel Cove, his narrowed gaze pierced my tentative armor.

"Actually, we're darn lucky to be alive," Brendan said. "The brakes went out on Jane's car. Good thing for the truck ramp."

Jedidiah nodded, lifted his cap and ran a long-fingered hand through his thinning hair. Something about the gesture bothered me, as if he was now trying to decide what to do with us.

"Yes, well, it seems as though you would have had your car checked out before you left the city."

I couldn't help bristling at his remark. "It's my sister's car and she did. I did."

Brendan squeezed my hand and shook his head slightly. I bit my lip against further retorts. The mayor seemed very different from the day I'd talked to him by Cissy's grave, and even from when he'd visited Aunt Mattie.

"You won't be able to get a wrecker up here until morning. I hope you realize that."

"Of course," Brendan answered for me. "If you could give us a ride back to the Cove, I'll take care of getting the car out of here tomorrow."

Jedidiah nodded, studied my car for a moment longer, then motioned us toward his sedan.

Back in Laurel Cove, a light rain began to fall. Once home, I put the tea kettle up and went to change into dry clothes. Brendan waited for me in the kitchen. When I rejoined him, he handed me a mug of steaming tea and a plate with scrambled eggs and toast.

"Old Jedidiah didn't seem in a very good mood tonight." He brought a plate for himself to the table and sat beside me.

"Old Jedidiah is a grumpy old man," I said.

Brendan laughed softly, then suddenly leaned over and kissed me for a long time. When he finally drew away, I was breathless, drifting in a place where nothing else mattered but his touch. I sighed and leaned my forehead against his. His hand skimmed through my hair and rested at the back of my neck, his fingers massaging the knotted muscles.

"Ah, Ceely Jane," he murmured. "Seems as though your plan for rest and relaxation has seriously gone awry. After all that's happened, you probably wish you'd never come back to Laurel Cove."

Did I? I had done everything but relax these past

days, and yet I felt no regret. If I hadn't come back to the Cove, I wouldn't have known this moment of sheer bliss, wouldn't have known what it was like to have Brendan hold me.

His lips brushed my cheek and forehead before he moved away.

"Best eat up. I'm going to leave soon as I see you clean your plate."

"To go where?" I took a generous forkful of scrambled eggs, savoring the melted cheese he'd added to them. "You do remember you have a flat tire, and it's a little dark to be changing it now."

"I thought I'd walk over to the resort and see if Theo will give me a ride home."

I put my fork down and stared at my plate. "I'd rather they didn't know what happened. They've enough to worry about with all that's been going on lately. I told them we might be late and I'd just leave Pepper there for the night."

"I suppose you're right. I'll just walk to my place. It's not far and…"

Outside, the rain began to fall harder, drumming on the roof of the farmhouse.

"Stay here," I said softly. "I…really don't want to be alone."

He said nothing but picked up his fork and attacked his food. We finished eating in silence. When I stood to put our plates in the sink, he took my hand and locked our fingers together.

"I'll stay, but I'll bunk down here on the sofa. It's best for now."

I didn't ask him why. When we'd washed the few dishes, I went for sheets, pillow and a blanket. Brendan took them from me at the foot of the stairs.

"I can manage," he assured me. "I think you need some rest."

I sensed he was purposely putting space between us, and though I really wanted nothing more than to have him near, I turned and went back up the stairs.

Was it a subconscious reaction to the accident that made me dream again? The realization I'd come very close to joining the ranks of Gran and Daddy and Cissy Oliver? I saw them all as plainly as if they'd been right in front of me. Daddy's strong, handsome face. Gran's powdery, lined one. Cissy's ethereal, as if in another-world. Seeing them this way, so real I could almost feel my father's big warm hands, Gran's frail blue-veined ones, Cissy's cool light touch, lent a strange reality to the dream. As if perhaps it was not a dream at all but by some trick of mind or time, an actual scenario.

They were calling to me. *Laurel. Look for the laurel. You must find it. You must.* The voices drifted in and out, louder, softer, closer, farther away. And then a popping sound ended them all.

I awoke with a jolt and lay staring up at the fine cracks in the plaster ceiling. My heart pounded in my chest, as I once again tried to separate the dream from reality. What did the dream mean? Why should I look for the laurel? What was the popping sound?

Tossing aside the covers, I went to the windows, shivering in my nightshirt. Without Pepper's comforting little presence, a sudden loneliness tugged at me. Downstairs, Brendan slept and I ached to know he was so close and yet...

"Jane, honey, are you okay?"

Suddenly, he was there beside me and without any

hesitation I turned and melted against him. He enclosed me in his arms, and I realized then how I was trembling.

"I heard you call out. Is it the dreams again?" His voice vibrated in my ear while his hands rubbed up and down my back.

"I…I don't know. It must have been, but it was so real. I saw them, Brendan! My family and Cissy and then there was a…a sound. It woke me. Am I really going crazy?"

He set me back a little and lifted my chin so I had to look at him.

"You most assuredly are not. Someone was just setting off fireworks in the Cove."

I sniffled. "In the rain?"

He shrugged. "Heck yeah. You know they like to get a head start on the 4th of July around here."

"But the voices…the faces…"

"It was just a dream." His voice was soft but firm. "You've got to remember that."

"But why are they haunting me? What do they want?" Hot tears of frustration suddenly spilled down my face. "I don't know the answer."

Before I could dissolve into a sobbing mess, Brendan took my hands into his. "Let's go downstairs. I'll make you some tea."

That almost made me laugh. Tea always seemed his best solution to my problems. And in that moment, I knew this time it was not. Stretching up on my tiptoes, I pressed my lips to his. His response sent a flame of fire through me and chased away the lingering chill.

"I'm not sure this is the best idea," he murmured against my mouth.

"It's the best one I can think of." I slipped my fingers

into his hair and felt his arms tighten around me once more. "And maybe that's why that old four-poster is still here in this room."

He lifted me and took me to it then and kissed away the tears. For the remainder of that night no dreams of Gran or Cissy haunted me, but I knew the memories Brendan and I made tonight would stay in my heart forever.

The terrors and uncertainties of the last few months slipped away and only the sweet yet fiery touches we shared filled my mind. In truth, I had never imagined Brendan would be such a gentle and generous lover, would give me everything I asked for...and more. And in the end, that he would take me to places I never imagined I could go. Drifting in the world he created, I knew it was a place I wanted to stay forever, where he was always with me, where we'd always be together, and that nights like this would never end. That when I turned in the night, he would be there.

Later, when we lay together, my cheek pressed to his chest, I recalled how back as a high school freshman, even though as an upperclassman he had teased me, I had often wondered what it would be like to make love with Brendan McGarren. Did I dare tell him that?

When I did, he laughed, drew me up, and kissed me soundly. "So now that you know, do I live up to your expectations?"

I traced my fingers across his lips. "Maybe. I guess it will have to happen a few more times before I make up my mind."

"Fickle woman," he teased and then proceeded to give me more on which to make my decision.

Before dawn I awoke. Brendan's arm lay across me,

and when I moved away, he only turned over and slumbered on. I got up, found my nightshirt and slipped it over my head. Going to the window, I saw the rain had stopped, but night still hovered with no moon to light the yard below. Mist clung like ghostly fingers to every tree branch and bush. Yet what did I see moving between the old maples? Surely no bunny this time. Could it be Gil again, prowling around? Did the man never stay home?

I almost returned to the bed to shake Brendan awake. Then the wind blew through the maples, stirring the branches, and the shadow became only a part of them.

Unable to return to sleep, I sat watching those branches moving in time to the wind. All too soon reality returned, and I began thinking about the puzzling dream and the words of the people in it. *Laurel, look for the laurel.* Whatever could it mean?

There was only one way to find out. Tomorrow, I would return to the cabin.

Chapter 12

When I reached the cabin this time, it was almost like coming home. Strange how fond I'd become of the ramshackle little place after only a few visits.

Had I told Brendan of my plan to come here again, he surely would have insisted Aunt Mattie keep watch over me while he saw to having the car towed out of the mountains. I'd said I needed to work on my manuscript and would spend the day at home. Satisfied I would be fine, he'd left me doing breakfast dishes. As soon as he'd changed the tire on his vehicle and left, I'd set out for the cabin. After the events of the past few days, it would be comforting to sit in the small armless rocker and just listen to the silence.

But the sight that greeted me when I pushed open the creaking door was no comfort. My first thought was tubing kids, looking for a place to party, had invaded Cissy's home. Apparently, they hadn't heard the stories of the cabin being haunted or else they didn't believe in ghosts.

Shocked and furious, I closed the door behind me and stared at the mess. If they were going to party, they could have at least not gotten rowdy. I finally forced myself to move, righting the little rocker and the wobbly table and chair. The key wind clock tipped precariously on the fireplace mantel. I straightened it. It seemed not a single object had been left undisturbed in the main room of the cabin, but my outrage changed to bewilderment when I went into Cissy's bedroom. Whoever had been in Cissy's home hadn't been partying at all.

The round mirror lay on the floor, shattered into silvered fragments. The drawers of the cherry wood highboy stood open, the few articles they contained hung out in vicious disarray. The faded patchwork quilt was torn from the bed and trailed on the floor. The corn shuck mattress sat askew; its yellowed muslin sheets ripped apart to reveal the course tick underneath. It was almost as if the intruders had been…looking for something?

There certainly could be nothing of value in the cabin. I doubted if poor Cissy in her whole life had ever owned anything valuable. But why would someone come into the cabin now and turn everything upside down?

While I straightened things as best I could, I considered reporting the vandalism to the mayor; but after last night's encounter with the man, I really didn't want to talk to him again.

I sat for a while in the little rocker, wondering if I might catch the scent of mountain laurel, but Cissy didn't come that day. Maybe it just hurt her too much to know what had been done to her home. When I left, I pulled the door closed tight behind me.

I paused a moment on the slanting stoop. Far off, a crow cawed raucously; closer by, a mourning dove cooed. Another sound, a soft scurry of little feet, drew my attention to the tangled patch that had been Cissy's herb garden. Before my heart could skip, I spotted a small squirrel scampering across the clearing and into the woods.

"Get a grip," I told myself and tried to obey. It was

finding the cabin in such disarray that had me so suddenly shaky. It must also be the reason why I was reluctant to walk back through the woods alone.

Putting it off, I wandered over to the garden and paused to savor the pungent odor of lavender, rosemary and thyme. They grew, even though Cissy was gone. She had once lovingly tended this garden, as did many a mountain woman, using the herbs to brew medicinal teas and poultices, and to flavor often plain meals. Folk medicine using cultivated herbs was a tradition of old, an art still practiced in many parts of the mountains. So why had Cissy's tending to such a garden been reason to call her a witch? Perhaps it had only been an easy excuse, a logical explanation for her eccentricity. I didn't for one minute believe she'd been anything but a tragic, vulnerable woman, a woman terribly hurt by life's cruel twists. She certainly hadn't been evil.

But as I stood by Cissy's garden, I felt something different about it. As if there were another reason for its existence.

I moved to pluck a bit of the lavender to take home with me and was surprised when my foot struck an object hidden beneath the tangled plants. A rock?

I crouched to take a closer look and discovered a plain stone, perhaps a foot wide by six inches thick, oval in shape, pinkish-gray in color; a native stone like any other one might find along the dirt road or in the woods. Except what was it doing here in Cissy's herb garden? And sitting atop a slightly mounded bit of earth that somehow resembled…a grave?

A chill settled over my shoulders. I stood quickly to rub it away. It was only a small stone, a small mound of earth. For a pet, perhaps? That was it. Cissy had once buried one of her innumerable cats here. It must have been a special one to have marked its grave this way, but it didn't surprise me. Old ladies, especially lonely ones, often became very fond of an animal. Cissy had been fond of this one; she'd buried it here in her precious herb garden and marked it with this stone. Only one more hurt and loss in a life touched by so much pain.

I left the garden and walked to the road. I stopped once and turned back to listen. Had I heard some other sound at the edge of the woods? Seen some covert movement? No, there was nothing, nothing but the hushed whisper of a breeze in the branches of the tall oak trees.

Just as I reached the end of the dirt road, I heard the low purr of a car's motor and turning around was surprised to see the mayor driving slowly toward me. There was no other outlet for this end of the road. He would have to have been by the river. Checking out some rowdy tube riders? Perhaps the same rabble-rousers who had trashed the cabin and set off the fireworks?

I stood off to the side of the road so he could pass, but seeing me, Jedidiah Hamilton stopped.

He touched the brim of his cap and nodded to me. "Out getting a little exercise?"

"I am." Did I dare mention the cabin to him? He should probably know if...

"You ought to be aware some nonsense has taken place in these woods lately, not sure if it's local kids or tourists. Folks have reported seeing lights out here after dark and hearing odd noises. I'm sure you're safe enough in your grandmother's house, but I'm going to have to ask you to stay away from this road and that old cabin. Mattie told me you've taken a liking to it, and I know you're interested in digging up whatever you can about Cissy. Fact is, I don't think it's a good idea right now."

"I'm not sure I understand. What should it matter if I want to know more about someone who lived in the Cove for so long? You said yourself, Cissy was sadly misunderstood."

"Did I? Well, it hardly matters now. The old gal is dead, and it's best if we leave it alone. And I'm only thinking of your safety, Jane."

As he drove on, I wondered why my safety was suddenly something he was concerned about?

It became something of concern to me when Brendan came to report the condition of the car.

His face was grim when he sat at the table in my kitchen.

"Is it as bad as I thought?" I steeled myself for him to say it was totaled. What would Maureen say? I hadn't told her yet what happened. Furthermore, what would I drive back to New York?

"Doesn't take much for those little cars, but that's not the worst of it." He motioned for me to sit down. "It's at the garage in Pineville. I had them check over some things while I waited."

"What things?"

"I'll get right to the point." His steady blue-green gaze held mine. "The brake line had a leak in it."

"But we had the car checked over before I left New York. How could they have missed something like that?"

"They missed it because it wasn't there. If it had been, the brakes would have gone long before they did."

"So… what are you saying?" The question hung a moment in the suddenly still air.

"Someone tampered with your car. The brake line

had been cut."

"How…who? We could have been killed!"

"Precisely."

The weight of that one word numbed me. I folded my hands together tightly to keep them from trembling. I could only murmur, "Who?"

"Try someone who's out to shut me up, who hates the League with a passion and isn't above hurting someone if it's to his own gain."

There was only one person he could be talking about.

"Deane? You think Deane Kimball did this? I just can't believe he'd endanger our lives."

Brendan stood and walked to the screen door. He stared out into the back yard where Gran's roses were just beginning to bloom.

"I don't want to believe it, but somebody did it. Somebody who obviously thinks if I'm out of the way the League will lose strength and Harrison Enterprises will win out. I know Kimball wants them in the Cove. He's got money invested in it already, I'm sure."

"You're forgetting one thing. I was driving. If someone was out to get you, why tamper with my car?"

"It would have to be someone who knew we were together, who followed us or waited somewhere along the way, waited until we left the car. It was only a small slit in the line, a slow leak, but the end result could have been fatal. Whoever did it might as well have tried to run us off the mountain."

I closed my eyes against the picture his words conjured up. "Could getting that hotel built in the Cove really mean so much to a person?"

"To some people any chance to make money means

a lot, the only thing that truly does matter to them. I know I've made more than a few enemies since I've become involved in the League, but what really scares me is your being in danger. I'm sorry for all of this. Because of me you might have been..."

I went to stand beside him and took his hand in mine. Warm and rough, the touch sent a now familiar rush through my veins, and I raised his hand to press my cheek against it. After last night, it brought back memories I knew would stay with me forever. Did Brendan feel the same? Or was he really more concerned with what would happen to the League?

"Don't think about it anymore. There's nothing we can do about it now."

"But don't you see? I have to think of it, because until this thing is over, who knows what might happen? Who knows what else this person might try?"

"Then is it worth it to fight? Might it not be better to just let things happen the way they will?"

"I can't. I won't compromise what I believe in. But I think it might be best if...if we didn't see each other."

My heart thumped painfully. I looked up at him. "What are you saying?"

He cupped a gentle hand to my chin and stroked my cheek with his thumb. "I don't want you put in danger again. This issue might be worth the loss of a lot of things to me, but your life is not one of them."

"But what about you?" Tears stung at my eyes, but I bit my lip to hold them back.

"I'll be okay. And I'll be gone for two weeks on the hiking trip. Stefanie and the others are planning their protest in Pineville, so maybe after it happens the League will know more where we stand. It will be time for things to either settle down or really blow up."

It would also be time for me to go back to New York and be out of the way. Was that what he was thinking? That in spite of the way he might feel about me, in spite of what had happened between us, there was no place for me in his life right now?

I let him go without argument, determined to save whatever dignity I could. Later, I would walk over to the resort and tell my aunt and uncle what had happened in the mountains yesterday. They would have to know. But for the moment I just wanted to withdraw and let the hurt of Brendan's rejection die down. The problem was, I didn't know if it ever would.

Chapter 13

I went to bed early with the box of notebooks Aunt Mattie had given me. Perhaps reading my father's words would bring some comfort and take my mind off all the disturbing things that had happened since I'd returned to the Cove.

His way with words intrigued me and soon I was reading with another writer's eye, tightening a paragraph here, clarifying a sentence there. My mind began to whirr with his vivid descriptions of the mountains and their legends and an hour passed while I read of fairy folk and superstitions, stories handed down from one generation to the next. And then I came to Cissy's story.

Somehow, I'd missed this book the first time I'd looked through the box. It was different from the rest; not a spiral notebook but a slim, leather-bound journal. I ran my fingers over the smooth cover and a strange charge of excitement jolted me, as if I stood on the brink of discovery. Somehow, I knew whatever lay between the covers of this book would change everything.

My hands shook and even Pepper lifted her head from her slumber and whined.

"You feel it too, don't you?" I whispered and glanced about the room. It had grown dark, save for the small circle of yellow light cast by the bedside lamp. A gentle night breeze lifted the filmy curtains at the windows and sifted through the room, bringing with it the soft scent of the mountains and summer. We were alone…and yet we were not.

Just inside the journal's cover I found a pressed dried flower, a laurel blossom. Something stirred in my mind…*Look for the laurel*. Could this be the reason for the dream?

With trembling fingers, I turned the first page and began to read the faded script I knew was not my father's writing.

September 14— "I have met the most wonderful gentleman. He is Irish as can be, a fine dresser and so pleasing to look at. His name is Mr. O'Malley, and he has such blue eyes!"

September 24— "I met him again and his given name is Sheridan. Some ladies of the Cove warned me against seeing him. They say he is a rogue, but he was nothing less than a gentleman to me."

October 1— "He came to the schoolhouse today after I dismissed the children. He brought me a bouquet of late-blooming wildflowers and asked permission to come calling. As the school teacher, I should have said no. Folks here about won't be pleased, but how could I refuse?"

October 16— "I made dinner for Sheridan and we talked for hours. When he left, he kissed my hand. I thought my heart would never stop pounding."

The journal went on like this for several pages with Sheridan courting Cissy ardently. Then, as winter settled in upon the Cove, she wrote…

December 6— "I have not seen Sheridan for two weeks now. He is nowhere in the Cove. Could they all be right? Is he really a rogue who will only break my heart?"

December 23— "It will be a sad Christmas if I do not see him. I am invited to the Stuart's house for dinner, but I don't care to go anywhere. I will just sit by the fire with Pandora. She will curl up in my lap and purr, and I will have to be content."

December 25— "I am so joyful! Sheridan came today looking handsome as ever. He brought me the loveliest warm coat. It will be a blessing on my walks to the schoolhouse. I had made him a muffler, which he wrapped about him and declared wonderful. But the best gift was just being together again."

The entries for winter went in much the same fashion with Sheridan disappearing for several weeks at a time but always returning to Cissy, bringing her some obviously expensive but lovely present. In March she wrote…

"Sheridan has asked me to marry him. I would like it to be in June while the mountain laurel is in bloom."

A few days later…

March 16— "The school board came to see me today. They said I must not see Sheridan anymore if I want to keep my job. His reputation, how he makes his living, is too questionable. I don't know what they mean, but I intend to ask him."

March 18— "I did ask. At first Sheridan attempted to make light of it, but I insisted he tell me. He works for a man who sells illegal whiskey. He is the go-between, the one who makes the contacts with the still owner and the buyer. He does none of the transporting himself but leaves it to the ridge runners, as they are called, yet what he is doing is illegal all the same. I asked him to stop before we marry, but he said it is the only way he knows how to make a living."

March 20— "We argued bitterly tonight. I begged Sheridan to give up his work for me. He refused and left in a terrible temper. What if I have driven him away? I cannot bear the thought of losing him, no matter what other people say."

April 10— "Sheridan came back tonight, bringing me early blooming wildflowers. He begged my forgiveness and asked me to marry him very soon. He has promised to give up the whiskey business, though we will have to move away from the Cove. I hate to leave the children, but we will have a family of our own. I cannot wait."

May 5— "We went into the next county and were married yesterday. I have told no one but have been informed my teaching services will not be needed next year. By then Sheridan and I will be far away from Laurel Cove. Having him as my husband makes it all worthwhile. He is a more ardent and tender lover than I ever imagined a man could be."

June 1— "Sheridan is to be done with this business once and for all after tonight. We plan to leave next week, perhaps for Knoxville, where he will look for more honorable work. Maybe I can teach there. I must find a home for my poor kitten. I might ask Althea Stuart to take her. She is the only one who has not scorned me for loving the wild Irishman."

June 2— "Sheridan did not return last night. I sat all these lonely hours in my rocker, waiting, keeping a fire going though outside it is quite balmy. I feel so cold, so fearful. When will he come back to hold me in his arms?"

It was all I could do to make myself read the next entry, but I knew I must.

June 4— "The sheriff came in the afternoon to tell

me, but I already knew. Someone had come before him and warned me not to talk, threatening me with my life if I did. He was a scarecrow of a man, tall and thin with eyes as cold as death. He said Sheridan was a traitor to him and had to die. Maybe it would be better if I died too."

June 8— "They think I did it, that I discovered Sheridan's philandering ways and shot him and left the laurel blossoms on his chest. They have no evidence to charge me and had to let me go, but oh the looks on their faces! In their minds, I am already tried and convicted."

July 15— "I know for certain now why my life must go on. I am to have Sheridan's child, and so I must never speak of the man with the cold eyes lest he come back and destroy us. Only Althea knows what truly happened by the river, but I have begged her to keep her silence, too. In time she will know why."

I had to stop for a while and let it sink in. Cissy had been with child when Sheridan was killed. Yet in all the years of her being a recluse, there had never been any mention of a child in the cabin. What further heartbreak had befallen Cissy Oliver?

November 10— "I have kept my secret well. The robes made from flour sacks serve my thickened body. I pause to wonder how Sheridan would have felt about this child, but I cannot dwell on my sorrow. After the baby is born and I am fit to travel, we will leave the Cove forever. I do not want my child to grow up with the eyes of everyone upon him."

December 5— "They were born in the early hours-- two babes, so small, much too early. My daughter never cried, never opened her eyes to this world. I named her Althea and buried her beneath the lavender bushes. My son clings to life."

December 8— "I have asked Althea to take him. Her infant girl is only a few days old, and her husband is away in the army. She must tell him—everyone—she had twins. I fear it is my son's only chance for survival. Althea is the one friend I have in this world. I believe she will do this for me."

It seemed to be the last entry in the journal, and for a long time I stared at this final passage. How had my father come to have this book in his possession? Had he read it through? Did he realize the truth revealed here on these pages?

I drew a shaky breath and skimmed through the rest of the book's empty pages, empty until the final one. There were two more entries, written many years apart.

September 25— "It has been over five years since Sheridan has been gone. I still grieve for him, but it is some consolation to see our son growing strong in Althea's care, care I couldn't properly give him. He and the little girl Mattie are like true brother and sister. They love each other dearly. Sometimes Althea brings them by when her husband is away. There was news this past summer of a shoot-out between bootleggers and federal officers. Some were killed. I can only hope one was the man with the cold eyes."

And the final entry--

June 20— "I will give this journal to my son today. He has been to see me over the years, never realizing the bond we share, yet somehow, I think he senses a tie between us. He wants to write about the legends of Laurel Cove. I think he must know the truth first. I only hope he will understand."

The year was written after this, and I realized my

father had passed away in August of that year. Had he known before he died that Cissy Oliver was really his mother? My true grandmother?

I slid from the bed and went to the windows, needing to breathe in the fresh air and try to clear my head. But it was no use. Tears flowed down my cheeks. *Oh Gran.*

She always knew we weren't her real grandchildren, and yet she loved us just the same. She would forever in my mind and heart be my beloved Gran, and yet now I knew what she had wanted me to discover, why she had wanted me to come back to Laurel Cove. It was why Cissy had reached out to me, why I was drawn to the cabin in the woods…and why I must go back there once again.

I could barely wait for daylight and slept only in snatches. As soon as a hazy sun shone through my bedroom windows, I dressed and went downstairs. I had no appetite for breakfast but made tea and drank it while contemplating the wisdom of returning to the cabin. What more did I need to know?

Then I realized more than anything, I needed to know what to do with this truth I had uncovered. I could show the journal to Aunt Mattie and she would also know the truth. We could clear Cissy's name, so that she might rest in peace. Or I could keep my silence as Cissy had, protecting my family. Maybe by going to the cabin, I would learn what Cissy wanted me to do.

The walk to the woods seemed longer today, giving me too much time to think about Brendan and what he would say about this whole matter. Would he even care? Or was his work too important to him for anything else to truly have meaning? If he had his way, we would not see each other again, but perhaps it was for the best. We had our own lives to live and they could not be more different. Too different to ever be compatible.

I was trying to convince myself of this when I reached the cabin. Sunlight had not yet filtered through the thick canopy of trees and everything seemed cast in shadow, the cabin suddenly emptier than ever, the woods silent. A tiny shiver of apprehension stole over me, prickling my arms. Yet I made myself go to the lavender bushes where the stone lay. I crouched down this time and pushed aside the tangle of growth. And this time I read the words crudely scratched upon the stone's smooth surface. *Althea—child of Sheridan and Cissy.* I touched the stone and thought of what Cissy had suffered in having to bury her baby here. Tears welled up for all she had lost.

And then someone touched my shoulder. A light, ethereal touch. I knew what I would see when I turned and was not frightened by the wispy figure hovering nearby. I could not see her face but could somehow understand what she said.

Must go. Must leave.

I thought she was saying at last she could go. Now that I knew the truth, she was free to cross over. I nodded and reached out to her, to my grandmother. Our fingers almost touched, then suddenly she drew back and, in my head, I heard the urgent words. *Go, Cecilia Jane. Go now.*

A sound near the corner of the cabin drew my attention but I saw nothing. When I looked back at Cissy, she was gone.

Fear hit me then, cold crawling fear that churned in my stomach. I began to walk swiftly back toward the road, but halfway there a figure separated itself from the

165

darkness of the woods.

"You… shouldn't have come back here, Miz Jane," he said. "He made…he made me watch you. Now he'll know."

I took a step backwards. "Gil?"

He nodded and came closer to me. I shrank inside but refused to let him see me quiver.

"You shoulda stayed away. I wanted to tell you. He made me watch you." His eyes shifted over me, and as always, he wavered, unsteady on his feet.

I struggled to get a grip on myself. "Who-who did?"

He didn't seem to hear me but stopped to listen to something else, a strange sound drifting through the silence of the woods. Childish voices from the past, chanting down the years.

Witch Cissy, Witch Cissy, say she killed a man.
Witch Cissy, Witch Cissy, name was Sheridan.

I heard them as plain as the day I'd stood with the children of the Cove. And now I remembered. Gil had been there too. Older than the rest of us in body but not in mind. He had called her name with the others but had been the first to run away when she came to the door.

He must have remembered, too. His squinty eyes grew suddenly round and terror-filled. His lips moved but no words came out. And then he ran, straight for the road, straight into the path of Jedidiah's sedan.

Chapter 14

I cried out a warning, but it was too late. A sickening thud followed the slide of tires on dirt and Gil lay silent, his body sprawled at an unnatural angle. I longed to run from the whole awful scene but found myself unable to move. When the mayor stepped from his car, I could only watch as he bent over Gil. After a moment he stood and looked around…and saw me. And somehow, I knew the fear Cissy had known when she looked into the eyes of Sheridan's murderer. Cold eyes, eyes devoid of emotion. Eyes of a man to whom life meant very little. Yet how could Jedidiah be that man? He would have been a boy when Sheridan was killed.

In a few strides he was at my side, gripping my elbow until pain shot up my arm.

"I told you to stay away from here. After all these years, you just had to stick your nose where it didn't belong."

I gasped as his fingers dug into my flesh. "Gil's hurt. Aren't you going to call for help?"

A strange look stole over Jedidiah's pointed features, his mouth twisting in a wry grin. "It's better this way. I won't have to worry anymore what trouble he's gotten into. My promise was kept long enough."

"Promise?"

"To my wife, who didn't have the sense to let me put him in the home where he'd have been safe. She was

Gil's aunt, and she begged me before she died to look after him. I did my best. I don't want to look after him anymore."

I struggled to free myself from his grasp.

"This is crazy. You can't just let him die." I managed to break away and ran to where Gil lay. He was barely breathing, and a thin trickle of blood oozed from his mouth. I wanted to get him out of the road but feared moving him could make things worse. If only another car would come along, someone on their way to the river. Where were the tube riders when you needed them?

I heard a click behind me and turned to see a small gun pointed straight at my head.

"I guess old Cissy was right," he said, his voice very calm. "You can try to cover up the past, lead a respectable life, but the truth is never buried too deep. What's in a man's past can't be hidden forever. Someday, it will catch up with him."

"What are you talking about?" I wondered if the shock of what had just happened was making him ramble.

He motioned for me to rise and with the gun following me I didn't dare refuse.

"We're going for a little ride, you and me, and I'll tell you a story. You want to know about Cissy? About who killed her wild Irishman? I'll tell it to you first hand."

He thrust me none too gently inside the sedan and slid himself behind the wheel. I scooted across the front seat and pressed against the passenger door he'd locked. The mayor pulled around Gil and drove on toward the river, steering with one hand and brandishing the gun every few moments in my direction with the other.

"Too bad you had to go snooping around. You should have left well enough alone. You and McGarren. I thought I'd be rid of you both, but things didn't work out as planned."

I stared at him, stunned to think what he meant. "My...car. But why?"

He ignored my question and talked on. "I hoped by getting rid of the old woman, nothing could stand in my way. I've invested it all, you see, my entire savings, in Harrison Enterprises. If it doesn't come into the Cove, I'll lose big time. I just wanted her to get out, leave the cabin and sign it all over to me. This is the most logical access to the river for the hotel guests, you see, and I couldn't have some crazy old woman frightening them away. But she wouldn't listen to reason, refused to leave. When I threatened her, she threatened right back. Said she was going to let everyone know what she'd known for a long time about me. I couldn't let that happen."

"What did you do to her?" Anger mixed with fear bubbled inside me.

"A little foxglove leaves in the tea. It wasn't surprising a woman her age would have a heart attack. They make digitalis, heart medicine, from foxglove. Did you know that? I take it myself. But too much of the pretty plant and... But I promised you a story. It goes back sixty-five years. I was fourteen, and my daddy was one of the smartest men this side of the mountains. He made a fortune in bootleg whiskey. He had people all over these mountains working for him. Sheridan O'Malley was just one of them, but he was one of the best at making connections, until he met Cissy Oliver, that is. She talked him into leaving the business, but Daddy had no intention of letting him go. Then Sheridan made the big mistake of threatening the old man. No one threatened my daddy and lived to tell about it…including Sheridan."

"And all these years you knew it wasn't Cissy who killed Sheridan?" It seemed hard to believe, especially after the way the mayor had made sure Cissy's grave was marked, the way he'd talked about her. "Your father told you what he did?"

His smile sent terror flooding through my veins.

"I was there, my dear Jane. I saw what he did. My daddy was a believer in teaching his son well. Cissy was the only one who ever knew, and with her gone my problems were over…if you hadn't come back to Laurel Cove and decided you had to know all about Cissy Oliver."

I didn't tell him I probably would never have connected him to the murder or the attempt on Brendan's and my life if he hadn't decided to tell me about his sordid past. It struck me that since he had told me, there was only one solution.

The cold steel of the gun flashed very close to me.

"I figured you might find something in the cabin, so I searched it pretty good. But I guess the old newspaper was the only thing, and nothing in it could incriminate my family."

"How did you know about that?"

"The old copy machine needs replacing. I guess you didn't realize one of the copies you made had gotten stuck. When I used it later that day, what came out but a copy of Cissy Oliver's face. Imagine my surprise. So I sent Gil over. He was supposed to look through your grandmother's house, see if he could find the other copies, but the darn fool couldn't stay sober long enough to do anything right."

We had reached the river. Jedidiah parked near the grassy bank. At the gun's urging, I climbed out and walked to the edge. The river deepened quickly here, and though it appeared to flow peacefully, the current was swift, and farther on those currents turned rapid. Was I about to encounter those rapids? Would I feel the rush of the water…or would the gun make sure I felt nothing before being plunged into the depths?

I had little time to think about it.

"It's too bad it's come to this," Jedidiah said. "You know I've always tried to take care of my Cove, and I never wanted Mattie and Theo to get dragged into it. But they had to let McGarren's group influence them. Why couldn't they see how good it all would be for us?"

"You mean for yourself?" I snapped, then bit my lip when he lifted the hand with the gun.

"I've watched the Cove get left behind time and again, while all around us people smarter than us prospered. I'm tired of being a small-time mayor, and I'm tired of people getting in my way."

The one most obviously in his way at the moment was me. He waved me closer to the slippery riverbank.

"Someone will hear the shot," I said. "There's bound to be a fisherman or a tube rider somewhere nearby."

"Chance I have to take. We all have to take chances." He aimed the gun, lifting it just slightly to align with my head.

My gaze darted about, searching desperately for an escape, and just as I decided, someone shouted.

Jedidiah jerked his head toward the sound, and I took the moment to leap, but to no avail. With one shove he hit my body with his own, and I went over the edge.

I heard shouts and a dog barking in the distance before I hit the water, and just when the river closed over my head a shot rang out.

The swift current tugged immediately at my legs, pulling me under. I wanted it to carry me away from the gun and the insanity of the man who held it, but when my nose filled with the green water, I fought my way back to the top, just in time to hear another shot fire and hit the water, then more voices shouting.

Blindly I struck out, reaching for something, anything to keep me from being dragged under by the vicious current. In a panicked moment, I realized I had a choice here of how I wanted to die—by the mayor's hand or the river's depths.

My hand closed over some wet and slimy object, a half-sunken log. I clung to it, choking but keeping my head above water. Dragging river water from my eyes, I searched the bank for Jedidiah's figure, hoping not to feel the heat of a bullet.

The voices and barking dog came closer, the yaps turning to anxious whines. Pepper's whine. *But how could she be here?* Then I saw her shaggy form trying to inch down to the water.

"Noooo…" the sound ripped from my throat. My little city dog would never survive the current. She mustn't jump. But before I could try to shout again, someone snatched her from the edge, a girl with raving red hair bound into a long braid.

"Hey lady! Hey there, hang on! We'll get you out."

More people appeared on the bank, maybe five or six, holding onto their inflatable tubes. The red-head passed my dog to one of them and grabbed a tube. "I'm comin' in. Don't let go."

In an instant she had bounced into the rapid water and came spinning toward me, caught in the vicious current. I held to the slippery log as best I could, my fingers sliding over the slime.

The tube nearly swept past me, but she hooked the end of the log just as she careened by. "Here, give me your hand." She extended her arm, motioning for me to let go of the log.

In that moment, realization hit me. *Stefanie.* The college girl I was certain had a thing for Brendan, and who hated me, was reaching out to keep me from getting swept away in the river.

I thought I'd known fear the night of the break-in, but even it didn't compare to the waves of nausea pushing my stomach into my throat. The hungry current sucked at my legs as she pushed the tube closer.

"C'mon lady, grab on or you're gonna get pulled under!" She once more reached out for me, and swallowing the fear, along with some river water, I let go of the log and latched on to her hand. She gripped it tightly and dragged me alongside where I finally gave one heave-ho to drape myself over the tube. Amidst a chorus of screams from the shore and a lot of kicking on our part, we managed to reach the river bank where several of the other college kids waited to pull us ashore.

While they dragged the tube and their friend from the water, I managed to crawl to the grass and collapsed there at the feet of my saviors.

"Hey, man, it's Jane, Brendan's friend!" I heard one of them yell. Then Jeff leaned over me and touched my shoulder. "Are you okay? What the heck you doing jumping in the river like that?"

Before I could answer, Pepper launched herself at

me and licked at my face, whining her concern.

"How...how are you h-here?" I gurgled before I remembered the reason for my river plunge. "Jed--Jedidiah--he'll--shoot us."

"You mean the old man?" Jeff said. "Nah, he drove off into the woods. But we heard shooting. Did he shoot you?"

I tried to sit up but only made it half way before Pepper pounced on my chest and more river water dribbled out of me, setting off a round of coughing. The kids just stood around staring at me, and I recognized them all as the group I'd sat with at Shirley's Diner. What kind of irony was this that they'd be the ones to save my life?

"I'm...okay," I rasped. "Not shot." *Just feeling and looking like a drowned rat.*

And then to my disbelief, I saw Brendan running toward me. When he got there, he dropped down and grabbed my hand while Pepper continued to jump all over me.

"Ceely Jane, what the heck happened? You look—"

"Yeah, thanks, I know." I ran my free hand through wet hair and tried to sound brave. I couldn't break down in front of these kids. I couldn't let Brendan think I needed him, but the truth was, at this moment, I did. With no second thoughts I threw my arms around his neck and buried my face in his broad shoulder while my body shook with sobs.

"He...was...behind everything," I finally blubbered. "He...tried to kill us...on the mountain...and me today. He...made the calls...to Aunt Mattie and Theo. He's been the one, all along."

He closed his arms around me and held the horror of

the river and the gunshots at bay.

Behind us the kids murmured while Brendan patted my back. When I finally could speak, I leaned away from him and glanced up to meet his gaze, his eyes full of confusion but burning like twin blue-green flames.

"How could he do it? How could he betray my aunt and uncle? How—"

"Save it all for later, Jane. Just, save it," Brendan murmured and first brushed his lips across mine, then pressed in closer for a resounding kiss.

While my heart beat wildly now for another reason, I heard a few snickers in the background.

"Hey man, I guess you know her pretty good. Will she be okay?" One of the boys hovered nearby, or as near as his inner tube would allow.

Brendan smiled against my mouth before he stood and pulled me up along with him, keeping his arm tight around my waist. "Yeah, I know her pretty good. It's okay now. Thanks, guys." He reached out and shook the kid's hand and gave the rest a thumbs up. "You can go ahead now, but be careful. This river is unpredictable in places."

"We know. We don't normally go in here but farther down where the current isn't so fast." This came from Stefanie, and I figured she was the one with the most sense in this group. "You sure you're all right?" She came over to us, minus the tube, and touched my shoulder, staring at me for a few seconds. "You know, I feel like I know you." She stared a second longer. "I mean from before that night at Shirley's. But that's crazy."

I tried not to slump against Brendan and stiffened my spine. "Maybe you've heard of C.J. Stuart?"

She stared at me a moment longer, then her gaze flicked up to Brendan. I saw the hero worship that still lingered in her eyes but couldn't be certain if any jealousy was mixed with it this time. Without looking away from him she finally just said, "Nope, can't say I ever have."

That stung a little but I forced myself to say, "Thank you, Stefanie and your friends. I don't think I would have made it out without your help."

She smiled and flipped the long braid behind her. "No problem. Hang in there."

With that she and the rest of the group continued down the path to their jumping off spot into the river. I shivered to think they had no qualms about it.

While Pepper ran around us, we made our way the other direction to where Brendan had parked. It was then I remembered poor Gil lying in the road. "Wait, Gil was hurt. Jedidiah hit him. We have to get him help."

"Already done," Brendan assured me. "I saw him first thing and called for help."

"So, he's not dead?"

"Hope not. Luckily, the EMTs from Pineville were close by. Gil's on his way to the hospital."

"Thank goodness. He was part of it, too, but he tried to warn me, I think."

Before I climbed into the four-wheel drive, Brendan held me back, drawing me to him again. I didn't resist but leaned in and listened to his heart thumping against my ear.

He stroked my back, sending little shocks of electricity up and down my spine. "I'm sorry all this has happened to you. I…feel partly responsible."

"How so?"

"This whole fighting Harrison Enterprises, I'm not sure we'll win, and it's hurting more people than it's helped. Most of all, it's hurting you and those I care about. It was never my intention."

I jerked away. "Of course, it wasn't! And if the hotel does get built, it's going to hurt Mattie and Theo and anybody else with a small business around here. I can see that now. So don't apologize." I lifted my gaze to his. "Just keep following your heart and do what it tells you is right."

His mouth crooked up in a half-smile. "What it tells me right now is this," and he dipped his head to kiss me.

Much later, after Aunt Mattie had insisted I get checked by a doctor at the clinic in town, we talked about it all.

From the corner of the sofa where I sat curled beneath one of Gran's afghans, I asked, "Do you think Gil will be all right, Uncle Theo?"

He twirled his moustache and shrugged. "He's in serious condition, but I think he'll make it. Mattie and I will visit him tomorrow."

I admitted to feeling guilty now for being afraid of Gil. He had never really been a threat, only a pawn in Jedidiah's game.

"What will become of Jedidiah?"

Uncle Theo's mouth turned down beneath his moustache. "I've known Jed all my life. It's hard to believe he'd turn against us all like that, and for money."

"Well, I just hope they catch up with him soon." Brendan had notified the police chief in Pineville, and there was a countywide search going on for the mayor of Laurel Cove. "After what he did to Cissy…"

Brendan came into the room with a cup of

chamomile tea for me. When he sat down beside me on the sofa and handed me the cup, he closed his hand over mine for a moment. "Don't worry, they'll find him."

And they did, not far from where we'd nearly careened off the mountain. Lost control, went over the edge, probably heart attack. That's all the paper printed, and nothing was ever said about his part in Cissy's death. It was my word against the reputation Mayor Jedidiah Hamilton had built up in the Cove over the years and would serve no purpose.

What did was the conversation I had with Deane Kimball a few days later.

Chapter 15

I decided to visit Shirley's Diner and finally finish a piece of that coconut cream pie before leaving the Cove. Mattie and Theo had driven me to town to see about renting a car to drive back home. Thank goodness Maureen hadn't been too upset about the demise of her car, in fact had used it as an excuse for her husband to buy her the latest model convertible as an anniversary gift. *Must be nice.*

While I sat at the counter, I listened to the background noise of clattering dishes, chattering voices, and country music on the juke box, while skimming through a few messages from Lydia. Once again, I promised to have the book finished in a week or two, when I got back to New York. After all, when I was there, I wouldn't have the distractions of everything that had haunted me since returning to the Cove. Haunted. Such an appropriate word.

One distraction settled himself on the seat next to me. I paid him no attention until I heard Shirley ask if he would have the regular and the now familiar voice said, "You bet." When I glanced his way, I met with those velvet brown eyes that were captivating even behind the thick framed lenses. Had he been anyone else at the moment, or I in a better mood, they might have charmed me; but today, even though I knew Deane wasn't involved with any of the threats, I was beyond being charmed.

"Hello Jane. Do you mind my sitting here?"

Though the diner was busy, there were other places he could have sat, but why give myself more grief than I already had?

"Wherever you like." I shrugged and went back to my phone, thinking I needed to check in on social media with those fickle teen fans of mine. But when I felt him peering over my shoulder, I swiped off that page and pocketed the phone.

"Sorry." He shifted a bit away. "Don't mean to be nosy."

I met the soft brown gaze again, and my cranky mood slipped away. Rather than his usual suit and slightly askew tie, today Dean wore jeans and a knit sports shirt with a designer logo on the collar. Not of the well-worn caliber like Brendan always wore but probably about as casual as the man got. *Why am I even making that comparison?* Piqued at myself, I focused on Shirley as she slid two slices of the creamy pie onto plates.

"Ah ha, I see you've gotten addicted, too." Deane reached over the counter and plucked a glass coffee pot from a lower shelf. He poured himself a cup and then held the pot towards me. "Need a refill?"

I pushed my cup closer to him. He certainly seemed at home in the diner and filled the cup before replacing the pot. When Shirley placed the plates in front of us, he wasted no time taking a huge first bite of the pie.

"Mmm mmm, best pie in the county, Miss Shirley. How is it we're so blessed to have you here in Pineville?"

"Just lucky, I guess." She patted her salt and pepper hair that was twisted into a tight bun and straightened her frilly apron. I noticed her cheeks flush a bit before she hurried onto another customer.

Oh yeah, he was a charmer all right.

We ate in silence, but when we'd both finished, Deane refolded his napkin and tucked it next to his plate, then turned to me. "I'm glad I ran into you today, Jane. Are you in a hurry to leave?"

I drank the rest of my coffee before answering. "Why do you ask?" I cast a quick glance at him, feeling the immediate spell of those velvet brown eyes. So different from Brendan's, and there I went comparing the two men again

"To be honest, I first wanted to ask if you ever found out anything more about the old woman who lived in that cabin?"

The question struck me and I hesitated answering. Not that I would tell him what I had discovered about Cissy, not when I hadn't told anyone else yet, but coming from Deane it was totally unexpected.

"I…did uncover something but it's not anything of great importance or interest." *Except to me.*

He pursed his lips and nodded as if he understood. "So, nothing you'd want to write about, is that right?"

I folded my hands to keep them from fidgeting. "Maybe…I don't know…I haven't decided yet."

"Well then, my second question is, if and when you do, would you allow me to print an excerpt in the *Gazette*? Whatever the story, I do think it's of interest to the community. Especially if…" His sentence dropped off.

"Especially if what?" I narrowed my gaze on him, resisting the charm. "The cabin is torn down to make way for the hotel? Do you still think that's going to happen?"

"I guess that's not for me to say, and with old Jedidiah gone, who knows who might take up the case for Harrison Enterprises?"

"Not you?"

He gave me half a grin and held up both hands as if to ward off that idea. "Not me. I've come to the conclusion it's not worth the hassle, and Brendan and I have enough in our past to feed the animosity. We don't need this, too."

I wasn't sure I needed to know what was in their past but found myself asking anyway.

"What is it between you two? I'm guessing it's more than being on opposite sides of the Harrison deal."

His brown eyes grew even darker. I detected a hint of pain behind their depths and sensed his hesitation when he picked up his coffee mug and drained what must be cold dregs by now.

"If it's none of my business, Deane, you may certainly tell me so."

His chin jutted out for a moment, then he shook his head. "No, it's…okay. Probably better you do know." He took out his expensive leather wallet, pulled out a twenty, and laid it on the counter. "My treat today, okay?" He nodded to Shirley.

When she hurried over, he pushed the bill toward her. "Thanks, doll, it was fabulous as usual." He winked at her and her cheeks turned pink again.

"I'll get your change."

"Nope, it's yours. Just keep baking that pie." He stood and inclined his head toward the door. "Can we go someplace else to talk? There's a little park across the street."

I slung my purse over my shoulder and followed him. When we'd settled at a picnic table near a stream that ran through the park, Deane stalled again, stopping to clean his glasses on a stark white handkerchief from his pocket before he spoke.

"Seriously, you don't have to do this," I said.

He gazed out to the willows that dipped over the gurgling water. "It goes back to when Brendan came home from the service and enrolled in college classes in Knoxville. I was just graduating and we barely knew each other, probably never would have met if it hadn't been for…for Kathy."

So, the bitter conflict between the two men had all begun over a woman. Somehow, I'd not expected that. Not sure it was something I really wanted to hear, I still murmured, "Go on." He told me then of the young woman he'd been involved with at the time. Apparently, the only reason he had started dating her was because her father was managing editor at a big city newspaper, and Deane hoped she might put in a good word for him if he applied for a job there. For Deane, it had been an otherwise casual college affair. For the young woman Kathy, not so casual. She had even gone so far as to tell her good friend Brendan that she and Deane would soon become engaged and planned to marry after graduation. When the newspaper job didn't materialize, Deane tried to get out of the relationship. He had been downright cruel, telling her he didn't have time for her, hoping she would turn to Brendan for comfort. Instead, she'd swallowed a bottle of sleeping pills. Brendan was the one who found her and got her to the hospital in time to save her life…but not her mind. "Kathy is confined to a nursing home in North Carolina. I've…never been to see her, but Brendan has told me over the years just how she looks. They had to cut her hair, easier to take care of, but my God, she had the most beautiful hair." His voice cracked and he cleared his throat. "It's hard to imagine." I noticed the nerve that jumped along his jaw as he tried to compose himself.

I thought back to the trip to North Carolina that I'd taken with Brendan. How he'd asked me to leave him in town while I went to the museum. How he'd seemed so quiet when we met later for dinner. I thought then it had to do with the folks he'd spoken to there, who were dealing with a situation similar to the controversy over Harrison Enterprises in the Cove. I was sure now he'd taken those few hours to visit with Kathy. Had he ever loved her, too? As more than a friend? I would probably never know.

In spite of the despicable thing he'd done, I couldn't hate Deane. We all did stupid things and sometimes lived to regret them. For some, the stupid acts lasted a lifetime.

"So that's why Brendan hates you and why you provoke him. You feel you deserve to be punished for what happened."

He offered no denial, only removed his glasses again and using two fingers rubbed the place where they rested on the bridge of his nose. Tiny lines of pain had sprung up around his eyes and his usually mocking mouth had firmed into a thin line.

"This is the first time I've talked about it," he said. "For years I've carried it around with me until sometimes I thought I'd vomit from being sickened by myself. And you're right about provoking McGarren. I believe I would have supported open sewers in the streets if it would have made him hate me more."

"Then are you really so much in favor of Harrison Enterprises? Or is it just another attempt to gain Brendan's undying hatred?"

"I suppose it was." He shrugged. "Though the financial aspect was attractive. I would like to have just done something on my own for a change."

Had I heard right? "Deane, did you say it *was* a part of it? Does that mean—"

He pushed his glasses back on his face and gave me a rueful smile. "It does. I'm backing out of the investment and encouraging them to build elsewhere."

"Seriously?"

He nodded and impulsively I leaned across the picnic table and gave him a peck on his smooth-shaven cheek. "Thank you. You don't know how much that means to me."

Mild surprise flickered across his handsome features, and he chuckled in a wry sort of way.

"If I'd known this was all I had to do to get your attention, I would have backed out of the deal a lot sooner."

A bit embarrassed at my own gesture, I felt my cheeks grow warm. "You knew where I stood on the matter. But does this mean you won't be antagonizing the League anymore?"

His wink was as sly as ever. "I don't know if I'd go that far. I mean, how else can I keep Brendan hating me so vociferously?"

Deane left shortly after that, and I drove back to my house in the Cove.

Chapter 16

A few days later we heard Harrison Enterprises had decided not to build in the Cove after all. A better site had been found closer to the hubbub of the towns. The protest planned by the League was canceled, and Brendan left with his students on their mountain hike. I closed up Gran's house once more and packed the rental car for the drive back to New York.

"Promise it won't be so long 'til you come back this time." Aunt Mattie tearfully saw me off.

"It might be sooner than you think." I settled Pepper in the seat beside me, still amazed the rag mop had actually helped Brendan find me by the river. "I've decided to keep the house."

She patted my hand and kissed me goodbye.

When I left the Cove this day, I saw no dark-robed figure alongside the road. I hadn't yet shared with anyone the truth I'd found in Cissy's journal, but it was known to me. It was enough to give her peace. And in time I would decide what to do with the story.

Once in New York, I tried to settle down and finally did manage to finish my manuscript. Then I sent it off to Lydia and found someone to sublease the apartment. The decision was an easy one to make. I found myself longing too much for the mountains and their mists and the stories my father had left unfinished.

The last steamy days of summer were winding to a

close when Pepper and I came back to the Cove. The little rag mop seemed to know just where we were going and watched anxiously out the window of the new shiny red SUV I'd bought for the first glimpse of the Smoky Mountains. I knew now the reason for my returning to the Cove and what I wanted to do. I would finish the book my father had started, and in it I would tell the story of Cissy and Sheridan O'Malley.

Autumn was no less busy a season in the Cove, and I'd promised Aunt Mattie and Uncle Theo I would work for them at the resort. I had yet to show them the journal; Cissy's secret was one I kept in my heart. But when the time was right...

Gil had recuperated and was now in treatment for alcohol addiction. Uncle Theo promised the handyman he would still have his job when he came home.

A few days after I returned, Brendan came to my door. Other than the few text messages we'd exchanged in the past few weeks, we hadn't talked, and for a moment we didn't know what to say now. Then he held up the picnic basket in his hand.

"How about a drive into the mountains? I know a good spot for a picnic."

Cissy's story beckoned me, but Brendan's offer beckoned louder. Besides, I still needed some answers.

I waited until we'd eaten and settled back side by side on the blanket to watch the wisps of mists rolling down the mountainsides to ask my first question.

"That day we went to North Carolina, did you go to see Kathy?"

His silence spoke volumes. Would he tell me the truth about her, or would I have to rely on what Deane had told me?

Brendan finally propped himself up on one elbow and gazed down at me. "Who told you about Kathy?"

I stared up into the turquoise eyes that could easily burn a blue fire right through me. "It shouldn't matter, but it was Deane. He confessed what a jerk he was and how it led to tragedy. I'm sorry that happened." I reached up and touched his beard, running my fingers over the soft bristles. "That must have been a terrible time for both of you."

Surprised he didn't deny that Deane felt any remorse, I rested my palm against Brendan's cheek, then my heart skipped a few beats when he turned his face to press a kiss into my hand.

"It was," he murmured the words against my skin. "And I did go see her that day." He moved away and flopped on his back again with his eyes closed, I thought to hide the pain. "Kathy was a sweet girl, but she let herself get drawn in by Deane's charm. Nothing I said to her would make her see him for who he was. Then it was too late."

"He carries the burden of guilt," I offered.

"Yeah, maybe, but that doesn't change anything. Her life is still over. Kathy's father's job took him to another state a few years ago. I promised them I'd look in on her whenever I could, just to let them know how she's doing. She is their only child."

I heard the sadness that choked those words. Would a lesser man have taken on that responsibility? Knowing Brendan had done so sent a rush of admiration flowing through me and I knew then that what I knew about Kathy was all I needed to know.

In a little while I said, "There's one more question I have to ask you. How…how did you know where to find me that day…at the river?"

He cleared his throat, locked his hands behind his head, and stared up at a patch of clear blue sky. "Well, when I stopped by your house, Pepper wouldn't let me leave without her. It wasn't hard to guess where you'd gone. You were so obsessed with Cissy's cabin."

"But after you got there and I was nowhere around?"

He seemed to be thinking, as if he wasn't certain he could say it.

"I saw Gil and knew he needed help fast, but there was something else besides your rag mop's barking that made me go to the river, even before I heard the gunshot."

Now I rose up on one elbow and stared at Brendan. His blue-green gaze met mine, and his wonderment matched my own.

"There was a woman. She told me to go to the river, that you were in danger. I didn't see her speak, but it was like I could hear her…in my mind. I was sure later I'd only imagined it."

"No more than I did," I murmured, knowing someday I would tell him the whole story. Before it ever became a book, I would tell Brendan everything.

Later, near the waterfall, with Mt. LeConte looming over us, Brendan asked if I would be staying in the Cove for good this time. I didn't have to think twice about my answer.

"I will stay, but I'm afraid you'll have competition for a while. There's this book I need to do. For my father…and for Cissy."

He took both my hands into his own and drew me to him. "If you can live with my environmental work, I can live with your stories." He kissed me for a long time, and for a while those stories drifted to the background. There was only Brendan and the sound of water rushing from the mountains. In this moment, it was all I wanted and needed.

"I think all of it can wait," he said, his beard brushing against my cheek and sending my pulse into overtime. "Just long enough."

"For what?"

"For Brendan McGarren and Ceely Jane Stuart to start a story of their own. We could call it 'Love in the Smokies' or 'How Brendan and Jane Became the Newest Married Couple in the Cove.' Sound like a good idea to you?"

It was probably the best idea I'd heard in a long time.

A word about the author...

Lucy Naylor Kubash has had a lifelong love of reading and has been writing for as long as she can remember. She is published in short fiction and novel length contemporary romance, as well as nonfiction, having written a column called the Pet Corner for twenty years. She is a member of Mid-Michigan RWA, Grand Rapids Region Writers Group, and Women Writing the West. She loves anything to do with the American West, mountains and beaches anywhere, and traveling whenever possible. When not writing she likes to spend time with her family and pets. www.lucynaylorkubash.com